MAN OF MUSIC

Megan Amery couldn't refuse a request to accompany her actress sister's small son, Stephan, to Vienna to join his father, an ex-patriot Hungarian. On arrival, Megan was horrified to discover the house occupied only by a housekeeper and Stephan's uncle, Gregor, an orchestra conductor. Forced to stay in Vienna with the child, Megan soon finds herself in constant contact with the enigmatic maestro. But Gregor is haunted by his tragic past, into which Megan is gradually drawn.

BRENDA CASTLE

MAN OF
MUSIC

Complete and Unabridged

LINFORD
Leicester

First published in Great Britain in 1981 by
Robert Hale Limited
London

First Linford Edition
published 2002
by arrangement with
Robert Hale Limited
London

British Library CIP Data

Castle, Brenda
   Man of music.—Large print ed.—
Linford romance library
   1. Love stories
   2. Large type books
   I. Title
   823.9'14 [F]

   ISBN 0–7089–9772–4

Published by
F. A. Thorpe (Publishing)
Anstey, Leicestershire

Set by Words & Graphics Ltd.
Anstey, Leicestershire
Printed and bound in Great Britain by
T. J. International Ltd., Padstow, Cornwall

This book is printed on acid-free paper

1

It came as a shock for Megan to discover the door bell was ringing and probably had been for some time. Someone jabbed their finger against it quite ferociously. As the noise of the vacuum cleaner died away she glanced at her watch which told her it was ten minutes past ten o'clock and a Saturday morning. That, however, did not tell her who was pressing the doorbell with so much insistence.

There was no time to put the vacuum cleaner away, but Megan hurriedly pushed it into a corner and as she made for the door she pulled off the scarf which had covered her chestnut-coloured hair. Glancing in the mirror in the small lobby to her flat she patted in a few stray whisps. The gesture took only a few seconds, for she possessed little vanity and was often exasperated by her own appearance which resulted in a great many of her male students refusing to take her as seriously as she wished.

The bell rang again in a way which gave her the impression the caller must be rather aggressive so after a momentary pause, Megan slipped on the chain and opened the door only a crack.

'Oh, for heaven's sake, Meg, I'm not the Notting Hill rapist! Open up, will you?'

'Of all people, I certainly didn't expect to see you standing there, Vivien.'

Her sister was dressed with her customary chic, her blonde curls tamed into a sophisticated chignon. Megan never failed to marvel at this beautiful sister of hers. At any time of the day or night she was certain to look as though she'd just stepped out of a fashion magazine.

'Well, you don't have to kill the fatted calf, or anything like that, but aren't you going to invite me in after keeping me waiting out here for so long?'

Abashed, Megan opened the door wider. 'I'm sorry about that, but I had the vacuum cleaner on so I couldn't hear the bell.'

'Don't you have someone to do it for you?' Vivien asked, genuinely surprised.

Megan gave her a wry look. 'There isn't much point; this place is so small and I'm hardly ever in.'

'I know; I've tried to ring you on and off for the last few days.'

She walked into the cramped sitting room and glanced around. Megan followed her, feeling slightly bemused at this sudden visit.

'Well, I'm glad you've called. How are you, Vivien? It's been months since we've seen each other.'

'I'm fine.' She gave Megan a wide smile. 'But I have been very busy. You might be surprised to know your sister is very much in demand these days.'

Megan laughed. 'Me surprised? No. I'm not surprised at all. I've always believed you to be very talented.'

Vivien smiled wryly. 'For a while I began to believe you were the only one with faith in my abilities.' She glanced around again. 'This really is a very nice flat, Meg.'

'I'm the first to admit it's a bit on the small side, but it suits me, especially as I'm not in very often. You're lucky to have caught me.'

Vivien looked at her sister speculatively. 'Do you still live here alone?'

Megan slowly took off her apron. 'I did share with another girl for a while but she got married a couple of months ago and I haven't got round to finding someone else.'

Vivien grinned then. 'You don't change. I'm talking about men. Why aren't you married yet? I know you wouldn't live with anyone until you are.'

Megan laughed again. '*You* were the one who couldn't wait to get married. How old were you? Seventeen?'

Vivien shrugged. 'Well, I'm certainly older and wiser now, and you still

4

haven't answered me. I bet there's some young eager solicitor in the background just waiting to take on a mortgage and school fees on your behalf.'

Megan began to wind up the flex on the cleaner. 'You make it sound awful.'

Vivien plumped down on to the sofa, pushing aside a duster. 'It'll suit you well enough.'

'It's just as well there isn't any imminent prospect.' She gave her sister a mischievous look. 'Perhaps I'm waiting to be swept off my feet by some hot-blooded Continental, just as you were.'

At this Vivien grimaced. 'I wouldn't recommend it, darling. It didn't do me a great deal of good.'

Megan straightened up. 'Oh, don't pretend, Vivien; he must really have been something for you to go rushing into marriage within two weeks.'

'*Something* is just it. Hot-blooded, jealous, unreasonable — both of us. I'm pleading insanity, because that's just what it was. Take my advice, love, find that solicitor and cling on to him desperately.'

Megan gazed at her and then grinned. 'All right, I will, but not just yet.' She went towards the tiny kitchen. 'Make yourself comfortable whilst I make us some coffee.'

She smiled to herself. With Vivien talk always came round to men. She was for ever in love and she couldn't understand why Megan was rarely, if ever, in a similar situation.

A few minutes later she returned with a tray which she put down on a table in front of the sofa where her sister was sitting, glancing at the morning newspaper.

'I assume you still don't take sugar,' she commented as she tipped a generous spoonful into her own cup. 'And I left the lid on the biscuit tin.'

Vivien laughed rather harshly. 'Thank goodness for that! I just can't afford to put on any weight, especially now.'

'Why now in particular?'

Vivien took the proferred cup from

her sister. 'Well, my career is really looking up, Meg. I've hardly stopped working in more than six months.'

'I'm so glad,' Megan told her warmly. 'You've worked hard for years. Yours is no overnight success, but, I've always wondered, is acting as glamorous as you always thought?'

'I can't imagine doing anything else, but it is hard work, Meg. Make no mistake about that. The endless rehearsals, the hanging about, and afterwards the nervous exhaustion. You wouldn't believe it.'

Megan laughed as she sipped at her coffee. 'It sounds positively grim to me.'

'No, it's wonderful, but even harder is the actual searching for work, having to look my best all the time. So tiresome.'

Megan cast her a wry glance. 'That has never been a problem for you.'

'Oh, if only you really knew! What I wouldn't give to have your brains.'

'Nonsense! You've never shown the slightest interest in anything except

7

becoming an actress.'

'I suppose you're right.' Vivien returned her attention to her cup of coffee for a moment and then asked, 'Are you still lecturing?'

'Yes, I enjoy it.'

Vivien leaned forward ever so slightly. 'I just can't understand you, Meg. You could go into a private law practice and earn a fortune. Do you know what it cost me to get a divorce from Alex? And that was just *my* lawyer. Heaven knows how much it cost Alex.'

'I can imagine.'

Vivien stared at her for a moment. 'Well?'

Megan shrugged. 'Well, what?'

'Why don't you go into practice?'

'I happen to like my job, Vivien, much as you enjoy yours. At the moment I haven't the least wish to do anything else.'

Her sister looked peeved. 'It really is insane. You're the one with the brains and yet I must be earning ten times your salary.'

'I do well enough.'

As she put down her cup Vivien sat back and after a moment's hesitation asked, 'Have you been home lately?'

'A couple of weeks ago.'

Vivien drew in a sigh. 'How are the parents?'

'They're in good health, but they are concerned about you.' Vivien's eyes were downcast. 'You don't very often let them know what you're doing.'

Her sister looked abashed. 'Oh, I do, Meg. I ring them now and again, but whatever I'm doing, they never believe it amounts to anything. They've never recovered from the shock of my going into acting. A safe career was all Dad could ever say; you must have a safe career. I'm sure he really believes I'm working as a call girl.'

'Rubbish! They do worry, Vivien.'

She nodded. 'I know and I will try to ring them more often, I promise, but I swear if Dad asks me again when I'm going to give up this acting lark and settle down, I'll explode.'

Megan laughed and then, a moment later, sat back in her chair and eyed her sister speculatively. 'Now, Vivien, what brings you here?'

Her sister smiled sheepishly before fumbling in her handbag and bringing out a packet of cigarettes. 'Mind?'

'If you must.' Megan got to her feet then and fetched an ashtray from the other side of the room.

When Vivien had lit her cigarette she said, averting her eyes, 'I have the chance of a big film part in America. It really is the chance of a lifetime.'

'That sounds wonderful. How did it come about? Suddenly?'

'I've just finished a small part in a film here in England. It was good, even if I do say so myself. Anyway,' she went on, inhaling deeply, 'I met this producer, Blair Holman, and he wants me to go over to Los Angeles and make a test for a part in the next film he's making. It's a big budget film with lots of famous names.'

'I hope it comes off for you,' her

sister murmured. 'I'd like to be related to a famous film star.'

Vivien stubbed out the cigarette which was only half smoked. 'Well, it's all up in the air at the moment. I'm not the only one in the running, but,' she added with a smile, 'Holman is a darling and I've been seeing quite a lot of him lately, so you could say I have a slight advantage.'

Megan smiled wryly. 'I see. So when do you go?'

'This week — hopefully. Obviously if I'm not there they won't wait; someone else will certainly get the part.'

Megan frowned. 'Does that mean you have some prior commitments to prevent you going?'

'Not professional ones, but, you see, there is Stephan.'

It was easy for Megan to forget about her sister's son — her own nephew. Vivien had been married only briefly after a whirlwind courtship whilst appearing in a play in the English Theatre in Vienna. Alexis Davos was an

Hungarian emigré who, it appeared, was as impetuous as she. However, such romanticism could not survive the strains of everyday living and the couple soon parted. So brief was their marriage Megan had never met Alexis who, it now transpired, had aspirations to be a racing driver on the Grand Prix circuit.

Once the marriage had ended Vivien had come back to England with her small son to take up her acting career. Megan had no illusions about Vivien; she could be shallow as well as selfish, but she had worked hard and she had contrived with a little help from Alexis, to bring up the child without too much hardship apparent to the boy. However, Stephan was now at boarding school and as Megan rarely saw her sister anyway she scarcely knew the boy.

'Why should Stephan stop you?' Megan asked in surprise. 'He's at school, isn't he?'

Vivien grimaced and much to her sister's alarm lit another cigarette. 'The summer holiday begins at the end of next week.'

'Oh, I see. Then why don't you delay your departure a few days and take him with you?'

She flicked some ash into the ashtray with a jerk of her hand. 'Don't be so simple, Megan. How on earth can I test for a glamorous part in a film with an eight-year-old boy in tow? It just isn't done.'

Chastened Megan nodded. 'I see the problem. What can I do about it? I assume you came here for advice?'

'A little more than that, actually. I was hoping you would offer to collect him from school for me.'

Megan shrugged. 'I could certainly do that, but then what would I do with him?'

'Well, it did occur to me that you do have similar holidays to schoolchildren and I was thinking . . . '

Suddenly Megan realised exactly what her sister was thinking and she broke in quickly, 'Oh no. It's just not

13

on. I'm far too busy to look after a child who, incidentally, hardly knows me. Moreover, it's not fair on him. I may have long holidays, but I'm going on a seminar in two weeks time, and then there's my work at the Law Centre . . . '

'What on earth is that?'

'It's a place where people who need legal advice, but can't afford it, can come to get that help.'

'For nothing?'

'Of course.'

'And I bet you work there without pay.'

'Naturally.'

Vivien shook her head in disbelief and Megan said, 'Have you asked our parents to look after him? Dad's retired now and — '

Her sister stiffened with indignation. 'No! I once did ask them on a previous occasion. Dad wouldn't hear of it. Waffled on about my responsibility and if I'd thought about the consequences before jumping into marriage.' She shook her head. 'I can do without lectures.'

Megan recognised her own father's intransigence and knew he truly believed he was behaving in the best interest of both Vivien and the boy.

'You jumped to the wrong conclusion,' Vivien went on. 'I don't want you to forgo anything; all I'm asking is that you pick up Stephan from school next week and take him to his father in Vienna.'

'Vienna!' Megan exclaimed.

'Yes. Stephan is due to go to stay with Alexis later in the month,' Vivien added hastily. 'I'll just send a telegram to tell him he's arriving a little earlier than usual. After all, he does little enough for his son and sees him only once a year.

Megan still didn't say anything and her sister went on persuasively, 'It'll take only a couple of days. You can be back in plenty of time for your seminar. Naturally, I shall pay for your air fares and any other expenses. There's no one else to help me, Megan, and heaven knows it isn't easy bringing up a child alone.'

Abruptly Megan got to her feet and walked away from her sister. 'I have the oddest feeling I should say no.'

'Then you will . . . ?' Vivien's woeful expression immediately gave way to one of pleasure. 'Oh, Meg, you're marvellous! You really are. I knew I could rely on you.'

When Megan turned to face her again she exhibited no such joy. 'Whatever happens about Stephan you'll find a way to go, and I happen to feel sorry for that child.'

Her sister looked taken aback and not a small bit annoyed. 'I hope you're not suggesting I'm not a good mother.'

'You're not a bad one, which isn't quite the same, but,' she added with a sigh, 'I don't suppose I can condemn you when I haven't any children of my own.'

'You should have. Marriage is good

with the right partner. I was unfortunate; Alexis is as impetuous as I and it was the wrong combination of personalities. Oddly enough, I don't regret any of it. It was wonderful while it lasted.'

Her eyes grew misty, much to Megan's surprise, and then Vivien said in a bright tone, 'It will give you a little time to get to know Stephan better. I've always thought he's rather like you.' She chuckled. 'He's not at all like his father or me.'

Megan nodded wryly. 'Well, I reckon I owe him a little more than just a card and a present on his birthday and at Christmas.'

Vivien got to her feet. 'This is quite wonderful. I'll never know how to repay you, Meg.'

'You don't have to. I suppose I can spare a couple of days for my only nephew. You'd better give me all the details before you go.'

Vivien was already walking towards the door. 'Not just now. I'll ring during the week, when I've completed all the arrangements. I've got an appointment with my hairdresser in fifteen minutes and I'll have to rush.'

Megan followed her to the door. 'But your hair is lovely.'

'Oh, really, Meg, it's a terrible mess. Speak to you later.'

She waved and as Megan closed the door behind her she drew in a deep sigh, wondering if, after all, she had made a grave mistake.

2

'Mummy promised to take me to the seaside,' Stephan complained.

Megan was pre-occupied with attempting to get through the holiday crowds in the air terminal, but she looked down at the small boy who was at her side.

'Oh, I'm certain your mummy will do just that when she comes back.'

'When is she coming back?' he asked for the umpteenth time.

'I really don't know, Stephan, but you'll be enjoying yourself so much here in Austria you'll hardly notice she's gone.'

'There are no seasides in Austria.'

'Don't scrape your case on the floor,' she retorted and he lifted it higher as she shepherded him towards the sign saying *Ausgang*. 'There are lots of lakes, though. Your father might take you boating.'

'He does sometimes,' the boy admitted, but with no enthusiasm, 'but he always brings a friend along, too.'

'Oh? What's his name?'

'It's not a he. It's a she, and I can't remember her name because she's always someone different.'

Megan sighed slightly at the thoughtlessness often displayed by divorced parents. She had seen enough of it at the Law Centre to put her off marriage and children for life.

'I wonder where Daddy is?' Stephan mused then. 'I can't see him anywhere.'

'That's not surprising. There are so many people here. He might be waiting outside, or he might arrive late.'

They managed to get through the exit and emerged gladly into the sunshine. Megan blinked, dazzled momentarily. There were a great many vehicles outside and they waited uncertainly to be approached.

After a few minutes Megan said, 'Keep looking for him, Stephan. I've never seen him so I'd never recognise him.'

'Daddy is very handsome.' She didn't doubt it, knowing her sister's taste. 'And as tall as a giant.'

Megan smiled down at him. After a while she said, 'Perhaps we should make our own way into Vienna. After all, lots of things could have delayed him.'

The child looked upset. Most of the other passengers who emerged from the building were boarding waiting coaches so there was no difficulty in hailing a taxi.

When it was speeding off towards Vienna, Megan said in a bright voice, 'It's a lovely day. Much better than it was in England,' but the boy didn't answer.

She glanced at him, looking spruce in his school uniform, his fair hair unnaturally neat and his blue eyes sad.

'I'm glad your mother has gone away to work for a while, Stephan. This is a lovely opportunity for me to get to know you. We haven't had much of an opportunity before.'

He gave her an accusing look. 'You could have come to sports day, but you didn't.'

'If I'd known about it I certainly would have done.'

Not for the first time since collecting him from his school did Megan experience a feeling of guilt for not interesting herself more in her only nephew.

'Will you let me know next time you have a sports day? Then I'll be able to come.'

'Perhaps. Last time I won the long jump. When I told Mummy she was very pleased.'

'Wasn't she there to see you?' Megan asked in surprise.

'No.' His lips were tight.

'She is very busy working.'

'I know.'

'You're really very fortunate in having a family here in Vienna as well as in England. It's a lovely city.'

'There isn't really a family here; there's only Papa. And Uncle Gregor, of course, but he's hardly ever there and when he is I don't see him.'

'Uncle Gregor?'

'Papa's brother — I think,' Stephan answered with a frown.

There followed a silence and as the Austrian countryside and small villages passed by Megan ventured again, 'Do you like school, Stephan?'

'It's all right, I suppose — sometimes. The trouble is, none of my friends believe I am really English with a name like Stephan Davos. We're always fighting over it.'

'You really shouldn't do that because you were born in Vienna and you're actually half Hungarian.'

'Yes, I know, but Papa doesn't live there. He says it isn't a very nice place any more, but I can't understand why he doesn't like it. I like England.'

'Your father must have bad memories, Stephan. When he was as young as you there was a lot of fighting in Hungary. He must have seen some of it which is bound to make him sad.'

'Yes, I know. My grandfather was killed, and then my grandmother brought him and Uncle Gregor to Austria. It was very dangerous; they had to walk all the way.'

'Well, there you are. You should understand very well how he feels.'

It appeared the matter didn't affect him too profoundly for a few moments later he asked, 'Will you take me to the Prater, Aunt Megan? It's a super fun-fair and there's the most fantastic big wheel. You can go right to the top and see all the city.'

She hesitated before answering, regretfully, 'I would love to, Stephan. Perhaps another time, because once I have safely delivered you to your father I must return home.'

He turned away, gazing out of the window and Megan longed to say some words of comfort but could find none. It must be very difficult for him to understand the complexities of an adult world.

The countryside and hamlets had given way to industrial complexes and new blocks of flats. Before long motor traffic was forced to share the road with trams and Megan drew a sigh, knowing that their destination was near.

'You could try to use your time here to learn some German,' she suggested as the taxi edged into a wide boulevard she recognised as the Ringstrasse which circled the old inner city and was lined with former palaces, museums and theatres.

'I already do.'

'Then improve what you know. Speak to everyone in German.'

'Papa speaks to me in English.'

Megan sighed with resignation. She watched the crowds of people strolling beneath the trees in the sunshine.

'I wish now I was staying with you, Stephan,' she murmured. 'I'd almost forgotten how lovely Vienna can be.'

'It's all right, I suppose,' he answered,

'but I wish I were at the seaside instead.'

Megan laughed and took his hand in hers. 'When you get back to England, if your mother hasn't the time to take you, I promise I will.'

He looked resentful. 'I bet you won't. You'll be too busy. Grown ups always are.'

'If I make a promise I won't break it, Stephan.'

He gave her a doubtful look which indicated he was still not convinced. Then he pointed out of the taxi's window. 'Do you know what that building is, Aunt Megan? It's the Rathaus, but Papa says there aren't any rats there; it's the Town Hall.'

The neo-Gothic building went by as did the government building close to, by comparison built in a classic style. The taxi turned off the Ringstrasse soon afterwards into an elegant square with linden trees shading its central garden.

The taxi came to a halt outside a

building which looked more like a palace. Built on three floors, numerous windows looked out over the square. Two steps led up to a wide doorway which was shaded by a shallow portico.

Megan was surprised and said so to her nephew. 'Is this really it?'

'Yes. This is where Papa lives. It's very big. He has his own rooms and I have mine which is much bigger than the one I have at home in London.'

'I can believe it,' she answered wryly. 'What does your Papa do these days?'

The boy gave her a curious look. 'He drives racing cars most of the time.'

'It must be quite a profitable occupation, but I hope that's not what you want to do when you grow up.'

He cast her a scornful look. 'Of course not.'

The driver was putting their cases on the pavement outside the building. Megan quickly got out at last and thanking him profusely she paid him the fare plus a generous tip. Then, when she turned round again, it was to see

Stephan still inside the taxi.

'Come along out,' she told him, rather irritably, for it had been a long day and this was not at all what she had expected. 'The driver hasn't got all day to wait here for you.'

The boy obeyed, albeit reluctantly. As the taxi drove off she said in a more indulgent tone. 'You can take your blazer off if you're hot.'

He didn't and she transferred her attention to the fine facade of the building. It occurred to her suddenly that behind the facade might be a number of small flats and after a moment, feeling happier, she marched up to the door and pulled on the bell.

She was kept waiting for only a short while. A small, grey-haired woman, erect and slim appeared in the doorway. It was daunting that her manner bade them no welcome as her sharp eyes raked over them both.

'I don't speak German,' Megan said immediately before the woman could speak, 'but Mr. Davos is expecting us.'

'You are English?'

'Yes, yes we are,' Megan answered eagerly. 'Do you speak any English?'

'A little. What business have you? Herr Davos is engaged and not seeing anyone today.'

'He will see us,' Megan replied, fighting her irritation. 'My name is Megan Amery and I have with me his son.'

The woman almost drew back in horror. 'His son?'

'Didn't you receive a telegram informing you of our arrival?' The woman only looked more puzzled and Megan went on, even more irritably then, 'May we come in?'

As the woman stepped back into a narrow hall Megan followed, carrying her overnight case and beckoning Stephan to follow with his. 'Will you please inform Herr Davos of our arrival?'

The woman gave her a hard look. 'You will wait here. I will tell the Maestro you are here.'

'The Maestro?' Megan murmured to herself as the woman almost ran up the staircase, leaving the visitors in the hall.

It was then that Megan realised at last it was, after all, one house.

'She's new,' Stephan told her once she had gone. 'I wonder what happened to Fraulein Gratz.'

'She seemed surprised to see us,' Megan murmured. 'I do hope your mother remembered to send that telegram.'

'Mummy has a bad memory. Once she forgot to call for me from school.'

Vivien's bad memory was already a legend in the family, but Megan recalled it too late now.

A few minutes later the woman came halfway down the stairs and peered over the baluster rail. 'You, *fraulein*, come with me please. The boy, he stays there.'

Megan indicated to a chair. 'Sit there, Stephan.'

'But I want to see Papa!'

'And so you shall, but first I'll go and speak to him myself and explain the situation. I'm sure it won't take longer than a few minutes.'

Reluctantly he went to sit down, much to Megan's relief. If he'd been anything other than well-behaved she was sure she wouldn't have known how to cope.

The woman waited for her on the stairs, watching her with undisguised curiosity all the time. When Megan caught up with her she glanced back to see her nephew sitting on the chair, his legs dangling and his school cap in his hands. He was dwarfed by the high ceiling and looked so small and vulnerable her heart went out to him and at the same time hardened against Alexis Davos.

'Please, *fraulein*,' the woman insisted as Megan hesitated, 'the Maestro is very busy. You must not keep him waiting.'

Transferring her attention from the waiting boy Megan cast her another curious look. 'The Maestro? Who is the Maestro?'

'Herr Davos, of course.'

She turned on her heel and led the way up the stairs which were marble and uncarpeted. Murky paintings hung on the damask covered walls and Bohemian glass chandeliers hung high on the ceiling above her.

It seemed to be a very grand place, quite different to what she had been led to expect. Alexis Davos was an improvident emigré who had, as far as she could recall, failed to hold down any permanent employment. However, it did seem that Vivien had lived in a great degree of comfort during her marriage.

For the first time since agreeing to help her sister in this way Megan wished she had thought to ask more questions.

'Where is Fraulein Gratz?' she asked suddenly when they reached the top of the stairs.

Several closed doors faced her on the landing, more paintings crowded along the walls. Reflected in a gilt bordered mirror her own face stared back at her in bewilderment.

'She was married six months ago. I am Frau Hemmel.'

She marched purposefully towards one of the closed doors and threw open one half of it, but even before she did so Megan could hear the sporadic bursts of piano playing which, it was now evident, emanated from the room within.

Slowly Megan entered the room as the housekeeper stood back, and she wondered what she would find. It was an enormous room, almost intimidatingly so and must have taken up almost all of that particular floor. One window overlooked the square where they had arrived and another at the far side of the room, the Ringstrasse and the Volksgarten.

Persian rugs tempered an otherwise bare marble floor and, swallowed up in the immensity of the room, were a number of brocade sofas and chairs with antique tables and cabinets ranged round the walls like so many sentinels. Mirrors and paintings decorated the walls and when she looked up it was to see a ceiling painted with cupids and satyrs with scrolls and gold leaf in a magnificent Rococo fantasy.

Almost reluctantly at the sound of a chord she returned her attention to the man at the grand piano which dominated even so large a room. He was seated with his back to her and said, in a voice bearing only a slight accent:

'Come in, and close the door behind you.'

Megan hastened to do so and when she turned around the man at the piano stood up at last. The sight of him came as something of a shock even bearing in mind Vivien's good taste in men. He was well over six feet tall, golden haired and with deep blue eyes which seemed to be raking her mercilessly.

'You must forgive me for not recalling you, *fraulein*, but so few women who profess to have claims on me linger in my mind. However, I assure you, if we had met before, I would certainly remember you, especially if our relationship was so close as to result in a child.'

He seemed to be finding her presence very amusing and Megan's eyes narrowed. 'What *are* you talking about?'

'This child you declare is mine; Frau Hemmel tells me he is about seven years old. Well . . . '

'Actually, he is eight years old, and he most certainly is yours. I find your rather flippant attitude amazing, and more to the point this isn't amusing after I've travelled all the way from England to deliver him to you.'

All the time she was speaking he was watching her carefully, the amusement very much in evidence.

'Perhaps,' he mused, turning to glance at one of the music scores which littered the top of the piano, 'we might progress further if you will remind me of our meeting.'

With mounting anger she replied, 'We have never met. I am Megan

Amery, Stephan's aunt.'

'Oh, his aunt,' he glanced at her again. 'And who might his mother be?'

'Vivien!' Megan was wide-eyed. 'Stephan is Vivien's son. How many wives and children have you had?'

He slapped down the sheet of music on to the top of the piano, the amusement gone now. 'Why didn't you say so straight away? We have been talking at cross purposes. My son indeed! He is my brother's son.'

She drew back in surprise. 'Then . . . then you aren't Alexis Davos.'

'No. I am Gregor Davos. You surely didn't think me the kind of man who would be foolish enough to marry a woman like her?'

Her eyes widened again. 'I beg your pardon?'

He smiled faintly. 'I apologise, *fraulein*. That was an uncalled for remark, but to be confronted with someone saying she had brought me my son . . . '

Again she was taken aback. 'You

surely didn't think . . . ?' She gasped then at the implication of what he had said. 'How dare you?'

He laughed to her further discomfort. 'My dear girl, if only you knew the number of women who have made ridiculous claims on me. However, you have my apologies. I am profoundly relieved.'

'You behave as if we were not expected. Didn't Vivien's telegram arrive?'

'If it has I haven't seen it.'

She pushed one hand distractedly through her hair. 'Then may I speak with your brother? I'm sorry to have troubled you.'

'If Alexis was here I am certain he would be only too delighted to see you.'

'Not here! Oh no! Where is he?'

Gregor Davos shrugged. 'Last week he was in New York. He had signed a contract to put his name to some sports wear. Someone obviously believes it will help sales.'

'This is *awful!* What am I to do?

Stephan is downstairs waiting to see Alexis.'

He regarded her coldly. 'And his mother?'

'Vivien is in Los Angeles, working, and she asked me to bring Stephan here to his father.'

'That, if I may say so, is typical of Vivien.'

Irritably she retorted, her mind working frantically, 'That hardly matters now. Do you know when your brother is coming back?'

'I wish I could be of help to you,' he answered, none too convincingly, 'but I really have no idea. Alexis is not answerable to me and he comes and goes pretty much as he pleases.'

He sat down at the piano again and began to pick out a few bars, making pencil notes to the score as he went on. Angry at his couldn't-care-less attitude Megan marched across the floor.

'Can I have your attention for a few minutes, please? We're not talking about a bundle of rags. We're talking about a child.'

He seemed unmoved by her anger as he turned around on the stool and looked at her again. 'You really must understand, Miss er . . . ?'

'Amery.'

'Miss Amery, this is nothing to do with me.'

'Nor me, but it remains a young child is downstairs right now.'

He sighed with resignation. 'Yes, I see the problem. Well, the best thing for you to do is to take him back to London again on the next available flight. Then, when Alexis returns he can contact you there.'

Panic began to well up inside her. 'You just don't understand; I *can't* take him back. I have a great many commitments and even so my flat isn't suitable for a child. There is no room for him.'

At this he shrugged. 'I cannot have him here. As you can see this is a bachelor establishment — when I'm home, that is. It's not very often I assure you. I shall soon go to Salzburg for the Festival and afterwards I have many other engagements in several countries.'

'There must be some solution,' she said in exasperation. 'You're his uncle and I'm his aunt. We just can't pass responsibility to and fro.'

'His parents do.'

He got to his feet again, towering over her. Then to her relief he walked away to a table where drinks and glasses were set out. He poured from one decanter into a couple of glasses, saying, 'Would you like some wine?'

'No, thank you. About Stephan . . . '

He ignored her refusal and pressed a glass of wine into her hand.

'Come over here and let's discuss it properly.'

That at least was something, she reckoned. He walked across the room and when he paused to look at her questioningly she followed him to one of the brocade sofas and reluctantly sat down in one corner. When he was seated in the opposite corner, stretching out his long legs, he raised his wine glass.

'*Egeszségéré, fraulein.*' She looked perplexed and he smilingly explained, 'The Hungarian equivalent of *Prosit*. I am Hungarian by birth, not Austrian.'

She nodded, drawing in a deep breath. 'Yes, I know,' and then sipped the wine as it was something to do and she needed to collect her composure.

'I shall try to reach Alexis,' he told her, rather magnanimously she thought, but she did sigh with relief.

'Thank you.' Then a moment later she turned to him again and asked, 'But in the meantime?'

'In the meantime Stephan can stay here . . . '

She began to say, 'Oh, that is very good of you,' when he added, 'But only if you stay to look after him.'

Megan put the glass down sharply to find him watching her through lowered eyelashes. 'That's impossible. I must

41

return to London by tomorrow at the latest. I have clients . . . '

'Clients?'

'I work in a Law Centre . . . '

'A lawyer, eh?' He eyed her so blatantly then that she blushed. 'How I wish my lawyer was so attractive.'

His wasn't the first comment of that kind she'd encountered, but she was irritated by it all the same.

He gave a more curious look then. 'You are not at all like your sister.'

'No, I am not, and I'm truly sorry if you're inconvenienced by our arrival, but I only undertook to deliver Stephan. I must return tomorrow.'

He drank down the last of the wine. 'Then I'm afraid you will have to take Stephan with you. This house is quite a responsibility so Frau Hemmel cannot give him the supervision he needs and I certainly cannot. Naturally, I shall endeavour to find Alexis as soon as possible. I dare say it won't take too long and you can be on your way again.'

Megan sat there in silence for a while. Aware that he was watching her all the while she picked up the wine glass again and drained it. Finally, realising she was well and truly trapped by circumstances, she drew in a deep sigh.

'Very well, I have no option but to stay here, but only over the weekend. Is that understood?' She got to her feet.

He looked unperturbed. 'Perfectly, *fraulein*.'

'My name is Megan.'

He unfolded himself to full height, saying as he pressed a bell in the wall, 'I shall instruct Frau Hemmel to provide rooms for you both.'

Megan suddenly gasped and he frowned. 'Because I didn't expect to be staying I've hardly brought any clothes with me,' she explained.

He eyed her jeans and casual sweater before saying, 'That is no real problem; I have an account at several shops and you are welcome to buy whatever you wish.'

She stiffened with indignation. 'That won't be necessary, Herr Davos . . . '

'If I must call you Megan you surely will call me Gregor.'

Two spots of colour appeared in her cheeks. 'I had better get back to Stephan. He'll be very disappointed that his father isn't here.'

'Ask Frau Hemmel for anything you need,' he told her as she walked across the room, well aware that he was watching her all the time. It was not a comfortable feeling.

By the time she reached the door he was again picking out notes at the piano. 'Do you sing, by any chance?'

She looked at him in amazement. 'Only in the bath.'

'That's a pity. You might have been useful in arranging *Lucia*.'

'*Lucia*,' she repeated uncomprehendingly.

'*Lucia di Lammermor*; Donizetti's great opera. I am producing it for Francesca Lamarti at the Salzburg Festival, but she is too busy to be available as often as I'd like.'

As she closed the door behind her he began to play again. She couldn't help but smile at the outrageous notion that she might have become an operatic soprano, albeit a temporary and surrogate one.

All that had happened that morning might have been expected, she reflected. Her own life was usually quite mundane, but everything connected with Vivien was another story. A simple party once had turned out to be an outlandish affair, and now Gregor Davos seemed quite peculiar.

Megan reckoned she could endure staying for a few days — if she avoided Gregor Davos.

3

'Why isn't papa here?'

Megan came out of the bathroom the following morning to discover Stephan waiting in her bedroom.

'I told you last night; he's away on business.'

'When will he be coming back?'

'I really don't know. Your uncle is trying to contact him. It won't take long, I'm sure. Why don't you get dressed and then we can have our breakfast?'

His look was reproachful. 'You said you wouldn't be able to stay.'

'That was before I knew your father wasn't here.'

'You don't have to; I shall be perfectly all right on my own.'

His independence touched her deeply and she answered gently, 'I know that, darling, but I did want to. Did you sleep well last night?'

'No, not very well.'

Although Megan had slept soundly after the journey she answered, 'That's just because you're in a strange bed. You'll soon get used to it.'

'I kept wondering about Papa — because he's a racing driver. Mummy says he'll kill himself one of these days. Do you think he's had an accident?'

Megan silently cursed her sister's tactlessness. 'No! It's not possible. He isn't racing just now, darling. He's on business.'

She caught sight of her own reflection in the dressing table mirror, a grand affair of gilded wood. Her hair fell to her shoulders for once, softening the lines of her face, her dark eyes wide. She tried to imagine herself in the eyes of Gregor Davos, scruffy in her jeans and sweater. What was undoubtedly suited to her life in London was clearly wrong in so sophisticated a place as this and she vowed to buy some tailored clothes at the first opportunity.

Turning to her nephew again she asked in a bright voice, 'What shall we do today? Have you any suggestions? You must know Vienna very well.'

'Can we go to the Prater?' he asked eagerly, his concern for his father gone in an instant.

'This morning I have to call in at the bank and arrange for them to transfer some money from London and then I must go to the shops and buy some clothes. I haven't brought very much with me.'

His face puckered up. 'Shopping! I hate shopping.'

'But we will go to the Prater this afternoon.'

His face immediately brightened. 'Oh, marvellous! Have you looked out of the window yet?' he asked, running over to it. 'You can see the spire of St. Stephen's Cathedral over there.'

The Gothic spire soared above the roofs of the inner city and could be seen from most vantage points. Below her window, traffic passed remorselessly along the Ringstrasse, glinting in the morning sunshine. All at once Megan was glad she'd been obliged to stay a little while longer.

'From my window,' Stephan went on excitedly, 'if I crane my neck I can see the big wheel at the Prater. It's all lit up at night!'

'What exactly does your uncle do?' she asked suddenly.

Stephan seemed surprised at her question. 'Don't you know?'

'He's a pianist, isn't he?'

'He's a conductor, of course. I thought everyone knew that. My music teacher at school is very impressed. He says Uncle Gregor is one of the best. Once when I was here before, Uncle Gregor gave me some of his records.'

Megan was quite impressed herself, but she said, 'I think you ought to run along now and get dressed, or we'll have no time for that ride on the big wheel.'

He needed no more urging and she smiled as he ran out of the room. Then, thoughtful again, she untied the sash to her dressing gown.

★ ★ ★

Megan thought her feet might well drop off at any time and yet Stephan was as lively as when they'd started out. She felt as if they'd walked the entire length and breadth of Vienna, although that wasn't so.

The funfair at the Prater was certainly much larger than she had expected and Stephan had insisted on going up on the big wheel three times. The view from the top of the Riesenrad had been terrific with all Vienna spread below them like a relief map. Stephan then enjoyed most of the sideshows and rides. Megan was glad enough to let him if it took his mind off the respective absences of his parents.

Now she was glad to sink down on to a bench in the Burggarten in front of the Hofburg Palace. The gardens had once been the private preserve of the

Imperial family, but they were now open for all to enjoy and it seemed that the Viennese were out in force on such a lovely summer afternoon.

Stephan, whilst consuming a huge ice cream cornet, pointed to a waiting line of horse drawn fiacres. 'Can we go home in one of those?'

'Anything which would save us walking an inch further, Stephan.'

'You're not tired, are you?'

She laughed. 'Only my feet. Just now they feel years older than the rest of me.'

He laughed, too, and she realised sadly it was the first time she had ever heard him do so. 'You are good fun, Aunt Megan.'

She was pleased at the compliment but looked at him curiously. 'Why do you say that?'

'Because you take me to nice places like the Prater.'

'I can't be the only one. Surely your mother and father take you to nice places, too.'

His face screwed up into a grimace as he finished the last of the cornet. 'Sometimes they do.'

Suddenly he sat up straight, his face covered with ice cream. 'Oh, look over there. It's Uncle Gregor!'

Her eyes opened wide with alarm as she looked round, following the direction of his pointing finger. Sure enough he was strolling towards them, arm in arm with a willowy blonde with whom he was enjoying an animated conversation.

Immediately Megan took out a handkerchief which she pushed into her nephew's hand, saying, 'Wipe all that ice cream off your face.'

He did so with less thoroughness than she would have liked and then, jumping to his feet, ran towards the couple. Moments later he was leading them towards Megan. Gregor smiled, saying, 'Well, this is a nice surprise. Are you enjoying the sun?'

'The rest, actually,' she replied, glancing at the blonde who was returning her look with equal curiosity.

'Allow me to introduce Signorina Lamarti, Megan. Franzi, this is Megan Amery who is staying here with Stephan for a while.'

The soprano smiled. She was very attractive and far removed from the popular conception of opera singers.

'Signorina Lamarti, I am delighted and honoured to meet you,' Megan responded with genuine pleasure.

'And I you. How long do you intend to stay in Vienna, Miss Amery?'

'Until Stephan's father comes to take charge of him.' She avoided looking at Gregor Davos and added, 'Do you know my nephew, *signorina*?'

'Of course. We have often met before, Hello, Stephan.'

'How do you do,' the boy answered stiffly in precisely the way he had been taught at school.

The soprano laughed. 'What a delightful child, and how quickly he is growing! You will soon be as tall as your papa.'

'Aunt Megan promised me a ride home in a fiacre.'

'What a delightful idea!' Francesca Lamarti exclaimed.

'Would you like to join us?' Megan asked, feeling foolish.

'I would love it, my dear, but time does not allow.' She looked at Gregor with a great deal of familiarity. '*Caro*, why don't you join Miss Amery and your dear little nephew?'

'And what of you, Franzi?'

She shrugged. 'I shall have to leave you now anyway as I must see my dressmaker.' She glanced at Megan. 'Gregor and I have a most important function to attend next week and my gown is ready for its final fitting.'

'Then I shall walk with you to wherever you're going,' he insisted.

'No, *caro*. We are only a few minutes away. You have worked hard enough today. Go home and relax a little. I will see you tomorrow.'

He took her hand and kissed it briefly. Megan, watching, thought it a

54

delightful gesture and one in which more men should indulge, although she supposed with most men it would only look foolish. Gregor Davos was someone who could perform such old-fashioned gestures and look all the more manly in doing so.

With a gay wave of her hand which encompassed them all, Francesca Lamarti hurried along the wide path in the direction of the Hoffburg. Megan and Gregor watched her and when she returned her attention to him Megan could not miss the admiration in his eyes.

'She's lovely,' Megan said, feeling a comment was necessary.

He looked at her then in a considering way which was not at all pleasant. She had the feeling at all times he was weighing her worth and comparing her with Vivien.

At length he answered, rather heavily, 'She is indeed.'

'Who would think such a great star could be so ordinary.'

'She has no temperament unlike so many others with a similar talent. Franzi is purely professional at all times, and, of course,' he added with a smile, 'she has the voice of an angel.'

'Are you going to marry her?' Stephan asked with the candour only a child would dare to use.

Although it caused Megan to cringe his uncle merely laughed. 'If only she would have me! Come, Stephan, let us go and hire one of those fiacres and give your aunt a taste of old Vienna.'

Hand in hand they went off together and Megan, still feeling a mite discomforted, followed. Gregor was waiting by one of the fiacres and immediately handed her up. Recalling the way he had kissed Francesca Lamarti's hand she couldn't prevent her cheeks growing pink at his light touch. The moment she was seated, though, he released her hand and climbed up himself, sitting next to Stephan and opposite her.

'How do you like Vienna?' he asked

as the fiacre set off.

'Very much. It's just like I remember it, though.'

He looked at her with interest. 'So you've been here before?'

'Once before, when I was a student, but,' she added wryly, 'my accommodation on that occasion was not nearly so grand.'

'I am very glad you find my house comfortable.' A moment later he cast her a rueful glance. 'I cannot help feeling you gained a very bad impression of me yesterday.'

She began to demur. 'Really, there's no — '

'It's true, though. My behaviour was not all it should have been. In mitigation I'd had a difficult morning. None of it would come right, and then the surprise . . . '

She couldn't help but laugh. 'It's quite all right, but do many women claim to have had your child?'

'You'd be surprised what they say. It has happened before. Fortunately I was able to prove myself in another place at the time she claimed we had an affair. An audience of two thousand people is rather a good alibi, especially when it's three thousand miles away. Then there was a woman who claimed we were about to be married. She gave the time and the place. It was in all the newspapers, and yet I had never even met her.'

'I shouldn't really be surprised,' she answered with a laugh. 'Where I work part of the time, we get some very odd characters.'

He put his head slightly to one side as he considered her yet again. 'You don't look at all like a lawyer.'

'And you don't look like an orchestra conductor,' she retorted.

'White tie and tails would look out of place for strolling through the park, don't you think?'

She laughed again before saying, 'Signorina Lamarti mentioned that you had a special occasion coming up; did she mean the opera you're producing?'

'No. In a few days' time I'm conducting a concert at the Musikvereinssaal. It's in aid of children's charities. Many important people are going to be there, including the President of Austria, and afterwards there's to be a big reception and ball at the Belvedere Palace.'

Megan's imagination was caught by the thought of it. 'It sounds absolutely marvellous.'

'Do you enjoy music?'

She looked abashed then. 'I used to, but lately I don't seem to have grasped all the opportunities for concert going I might.'

'We shall have to rectify that whilst you're here. To be in Vienna is to enjoy music, which reminds me.'

He slipped his hand into his pocket and drew out an envelope which he handed to her. She gave it a curious look.

'Inside you'll find tickets for the next performance of the Spanish Riding School. Believe me, tickets are hard to come by. I thought Stephan would enjoy it.'

Her cheeks grew pink yet again, this time with pleasure at this thoughtfulness. 'Stephan! Did you hear that? We're going to see the Lipizzaner horses perform at the Hoffburg.'

His face was rosy with pleasure. 'When is it?' he asked reaching for the envelope.

'Tonight,' his uncle told him and the boy began to jump up and down with delight.

Megan gave Gregor a grateful look. 'He's been asking to go since we arrived. Thank you very much.'

The fiacre jerked to a halt and he jumped to the ground, first lifting Stephan down and then giving his hand to her.

'Stephen, hurry inside and get washed for tea,' she told the boy rather breathlessly as his uncle paid the driver.

'I'm not hungry.'

'That's not surprising after ice cream, a doughnut and a slice of

60

sachertorte,' she answered wryly. 'I can't help feeling your mother wouldn't be pleased with me for letting you eat all that sweet stuff.'

'Mummy always buys me cake and ice cream, and so does Papa when he's here. We always go to Demel's.'

She cast him an indulgent look. 'I might have guessed. Well, go and get washed anyway. You must be filthy after all we've done today.'

As he went reluctantly indoors Megan looked to Gregor who came towards her. Guiltily she asked, having quite forgotten, 'Did you try to contact Alexis?'

'Yes, but he has already left New York, I'm afraid, apparently for Monte Carlo. He has a small apartment there. I've left a message for him and I'll let you know as soon as I manage to contact him.'

She preceded him indoors and just as she was about to go upstairs she paused to say, 'Thank you for coming back with us. I think it means a lot to

61

Stephan. He admires you.'

'It was a pleasure,' he told her, giving her a frank, appraising look which immediately caused her to avert her eyes.

To cover up her confusion she turned on her heel and fled up the stairs in search of her nephew.

4

Several days passed with a surprisingly pleasant speed. Megan and her nephew paid several further visits to the Prater and to counterbalance that she insisted they also visit a few of Vienna's excellent museums and palaces. Although it wasn't what he really wanted to do Stephan did seem pleased to be able to show off his knowledge of the city to his aunt.

During that time Megan saw little of Gregor Davos. She did catch glimpses of him going out several times and occasionally heard him at the piano in the salon as she passed by. She felt she might like to converse with him further after their ride in the fiacre, for he no longer seemed as remote or as odd as on their first meeting, but the opportunity did not present itself and she gained a great deal of satisfaction out of the burgeoning relationship she was forging between Stephan and herself.

However, two days before the seminar in Brighton was due to begin she realised there had been no news from Alexis and she began to wonder what was happening, even though the seminar seemed not so important as it once did and Stephan no longer asked constantly when his father would be arriving.

One day, after returning to the house, Megan paused outside the salon before continuing up the stairs. There was no sound from within and she knocked hesitantly on the door. There was no reply and after a few moments she plucked up enough courage to open the door.

Gregor was not there, but Stephen immediately gasped when he caught sight of the grand piano. Before Megan could stop him he had run across the room to look at it admiringly from closer quarters.

'Isn't this a smashing piano?' he asked.

Megan was uneasy. 'It belongs to your uncle, Stephan, so you'd better not touch it.'

'Do you think he would let me play a tune?'

'I don't know. Can you play?'

She came further into the room as he sat down on the stool. 'I am learning at school. My teacher says I am very good.'

He began to pick out a tune, hitting several discordant notes which seemed almost sacrilegious and Megan felt even more uneasy. 'Stephan, you should really ask permission first. He might be very angry.'

'Oh, I am certain Uncle Gregor won't mind at all.'

Gaining confidence he began to play a simple tune which to her untrained ears sounded good for his age.

'You enjoy playing, don't you?' she asked, surprised.

'It's what I like best. I'm not very

good at other things. Shall I play you a tune I learned just before the holidays?'

No longer concerned about Gregor, she nodded, happy to see him so contented. 'Please do.'

His brow furrowed into fierce concentration and he looked comically small, sitting at such a large instrument.

As the last note of the short tune died away someone shouted, 'Bravo!'

The boy jumped quickly to his feet and Megan turned on her heel to see Gregor and Francesca Lamarti standing in the doorway. There was no way of telling just then if he were angry or not at their presence in his private sanctum.

'I'm so sorry, Gregor,' she began, glancing apologetically at the Italian woman who was immaculately dressed in a blue silk two-piece which exactly matched the colour of her eyes.

'Why apologise?' he said, coming further into the room. 'I had no idea my nephew was so talented.'

The boy beamed and Francesca Lamarti said, 'It was quite charming.'

He walked up to the piano as Francesca went across the room. She put her handbag down on one of the sofas and began to stare out of the window.

'Mozart was composing and playing concerts at your age, but I think you will have to practise a little bit more.'

Stephan thought that was amusing. 'It's a smashing piano.'

'Use it whenever you wish.' He glanced at Megan. 'It will give your aunt a respite from your company.'

He was looking at her with great interest and she knew why. She had shopped with a rare abandon in the boutiques of the Kärntnerstrasse and as a result the jeans had been discarded and she was wearing a well-cut silk shirt and tailored skirt. He looked both surprised and impressed, something which confused her and caused her to laugh rather harshly.

'Oh, indeed it would be a welcome change. I've been up on the Riesenrad so many times I'm beginning to suffer from vertigo,' she replied, relieved at his response to the boy. 'And we really enjoyed seeing the Spanish Riding School. I took Stephan back the other morning to visit the stables.'

'Can I play in an orchestra?' Stephan asked and his uncle gave him his attention once more.

'If you practise enough I wouldn't be at all surprised.'

Megan drew in a sharp breath before glancing at the soprano. 'You must have a great deal to do so we'll leave you now. Come along, Stephan.'

She took his hand and glanced once more at the other woman. 'Goodbye, Signorina Lamarti.'

The soprano turned from the window and smiled at them both. '*Arrivederci, signorina.*'

As they reached the door she suddenly recalled why she had come to the salon in the first place. She sent Stephan along to his room and turned back. Francesca Lamarti was studying a musical score. Gregor had just taken off his suede jacket and was about to join her.

Megan was apprehensive about disturbing them and when she approached he looked at her speculatively.

'I forgot to ask if you'd heard any news of Alexis.'

He drew a sigh. 'My brother is proving particularly elusive, I'm afraid. He is not after all in Monte Carlo. I have left several messages for him in various places so one of them is bound to reach him. In the meantime we must wait and hope it does not take much longer.'

'I can't wait any longer. I have to leave tomorrow because I need to be in Brighton the day after.'

He came towards her, looking concerned. 'You cannot go now. What about Stephan? How can you think of leaving before Alexis arrives?'

Megan's eyes took on a steely look. 'Gregor, you know very well I agreed only to stay over the weekend. I've been here a week! I believe that is fair enough, don't you?'

'I agree with you and I sympathise. It isn't my fault, as you already know. I believed Alexis would soon be located.'

'It still remains that I have a seminar to attend and it won't wait until I'm ready.'

He stared at her accusingly. 'Who will look after Stephan if you go?'

'He isn't my responsibility. I agreed only to bring him here. I believe I have more than met my obligations.'

'I won't argue with you over that. He is his parents' responsibility but the simple truth is that they are not here. I am quite prepared to provide for him but I am unable to look after him myself. Surely it is not too onerous for you to stay on just a little longer.'

Francesca was looking at them curiously, and Megan was growing angry. He seemed to believe she could serve as a nursemaid and to be dismissed in this way infuriated her.

Unwilling to give vent to her anger in

front of Francesca Lamarti, Megan turned on her heel and marched out of the room, knowing it was useless to try and reason with a man she knew to be totally arrogant and self-centred. His own wants and needs were obviously all he cared about.

Just as she reached the hall, however, he caught up with her and swung her round to face him and it was immediately obvious his anger matched her own.

'Where are you going?' he demanded in a way which did nothing to mollify her. 'I don't like people walking out on me.'

'What a pity,' she sneered. 'Why don't you just assume I'm a temperamental prima donna. I'm sure they often walk out on you.'

'No, they don't. They are too professional to indulge in such childish antics.'

'Childish! You seem to have forgotten I have a career, too. This seminar is important.'

'Surely not so important.'

'To me it's as important as a Festival is to you.'

'Perhaps, but if, for any reason, I cannot go something like two thousand people will be disappointed, not to mention the scores of musicians and artistes.'

She turned away once again, not caring if it did make him angry. 'I am already aware of how important you are but I am still going to my room to pack!'

His anger seemed to fade a little. 'Oh, please, don't be so hasty. I am quite sure Alexis will be here soon.'

'He may never be here, and I dislike this male attitude which assumes a man's profession is all important, and yet a woman's must be prey to the demands of a small child.'

He looked contrite now. 'I am sorry. I didn't mean to sound so chauvinistic.'

She turned her head away again in frustration. 'Oh, it isn't your fault or mine, but if that sister of mine were here now I would cheerfully strangle her.'

He smiled then and in the face of that her anger melted readily. She began to feel rather uneasy and her instinct was to move away from him. Just as she began to put more distance between them he caught hold of her arm again and drew her close. His face was dangerously close to hers.

'Megan, don't leave just yet. Please. I'm asking you most sincerely.'

In alarm she looked up at him as he took hold of her hand and held it in his. There was a genuine plea in his eyes and involuntarily she felt emotion welling up inside her. Her feelings were totally confused now and a movement inside the salon distracted her as Signorina Lamarti appeared in the doorway, eyeing them both wrly.

'*Caro*, I hate to rush you but we have so much work to do and I have little time to spare.'

He looked at Megan again, still

retaining his grip on her hand. 'Will you stay?'

Almost against her will she found she was nodding, at the same time averting her eyes from the almost hypnotic power of his. He released her hand at last and she moved away from him with a haste for which there was no real justification.

This time he did not stop her and rather dazedly she went in search of Stephan, wondering why he had so easily prevailed upon her to stay.

5

The hesitant strains of Stephan's piano playing were easily recognisable from the practised skill of his uncle as Megan approached the salon.

Now, whenever the boy was missing, she could be certain of finding him at his uncle's piano. It now held a greater attraction than the Riesenrad and that was something which Megan welcomed eagerly. Gregor was so often absent from the house the boy could satisfy his craving to play the piano as often as he wished, which left her with more time to relax, to read, and to write to friends who might be puzzled by her abrupt departure from London. She had also cancelled her booking for the seminar, philosophically assuming she wouldn't have learned very much anyway, an attitude which amazed her in view of her previous keenness to go.

Time and time again her thoughts returned to when he had asked her to stay. It had had such an odd effect upon her and Megan tried hard not to dwell on any significance it might have had. After all, she was only anxious not to be left in charge of a small child and she could understand his feelings on that score very well indeed.

She pushed open the door of the salon so as not to startle Stephan and was surprised to discover him sharing the piano stool with his uncle.

'Stephan,' she said immediately, 'you know very well you're not to come in here when your uncle is working.'

Gregor got to his feet. 'It is quite all right,' he told her soothingly, for she appeared to be somewhat perturbed. 'He's no trouble. I invited him in, in fact, and we're having an impromptu lesson. It's quite a pleasant change for me, too.'

She relaxed a little and came further into the room as he said to the boy,

'Show your aunt how well you're playing now.'

Stephan obliged by playing, to her surprise, a Chopin nocturne.

'That's really wonderful,' she gasped when he had finished.

'Not quite,' Gregor contradicted, 'but he knows now what he is aiming for. We shall have him as a pupil at the Conservatory yet. Would you like to study music in Vienna, Stephan?'

The boy's cheeks grew pink with pleasure. 'Oh, yes, I would. And then I'd be able to see Papa more often, wouldn't I?'

Gregor laughed. 'I'm not so sure about that.'

'I wonder if my sister is aware of his talent,' Megan said as Stephan began to play the piece again.

Gregor moved away from the piano. 'I am sure Vivien is aware of nothing but herself.'

She looked away at such an accurate summing up of her sister's character.

'She has no idea what she's missing.'

77

'I'm sure she does — and she doesn't miss it,' he answered, giving her an ironic smile. 'And if you miss it when Stephan is not around you should take note and do something about it.'

'I'm not sure I follow you,' she answered, giving him a curious look.

'If you enjoy caring for someone else's child, it is quite obvious you should have some of your own.'

Again two spots of colour came into her cheeks and he went on, looking at her speculatively, 'There must be many a man in your life anxious to make you his wife.'

'I do have a great many friends,' she answered stiffly, not forgetting their last meeting.

'I think your anxiety to return to London has little to do with work after all,' he said wryly.

Megan applied herself to listening to Stephan's piano playing, having decided not to answer his innuendoes.

'I'm sorry,' he said a moment later, sounding not the least bit regretful, 'I shouldn't ask such personal questions.'

'Oh, you can ask,' she replied artlessly, 'but that doesn't mean I'm going to answer.'

'I have it right!' Stephan cried. 'Listen to this, Uncle Gregor.'

He played a few notes and Gregor said, almost in an off-hand way, 'It is better, but not nearly right.'

The boy groaned but continued to practise as Gregor turned to Megan again.

'If English men indulge only in friendships then it must be true what is said of them.'

'Which is?'

'That they're cold and unromantic.'

'I have never found it so, but that makes me wonder what your opinion of English women must be.'

'Up until now, not very high, I'm afraid, but having said that I must admit the only one I knew at all well was your own sister.'

Megan cast him a sharp look. 'I am the first to agree that Vivien is far from perfect, but the break-up of her marriage was not entirely her fault.'

'Indeed, I would be the last to suggest it,' he told her apologetically. 'Alexis, I regret to say, is also far from perfect.'

She couldn't help but smile. 'Whereas you consider that you are.'

The anger which always seemed to assail her in his company was immediately melted by the appearance of his most roguish smile.

'Oh, I didn't say that. If I did, it just wouldn't be true. Perfection is only for the most boring of the human race.'

Her face relaxed into a smile. 'I have yet to meet anyone who is perfect anyway. Tell me, is there any news from Alexis?'

His lips quirked into an ironic smile. 'Still so anxious to leave us?'

She leaned back against the piano as Stephan asked, 'That was better, wasn't it?'

'Much,' his uncle agreed, still looking at Megan.

She gave him an arch look. 'I am reconciled to having a free holiday in very congenial surroundings.'

He looked more than relieved and she wondered then if this sudden interest in Stephan's fledgling talent wasn't just in order to placate her a little.

'I'm glad you find it so comfortable here.'

'You shouldn't be surprised; you do live in a fairly grand style,' she pointed out.

'It's an Hungarian trait. We like to live well,' he answered, picking up some sheets of music from the piano top. 'When we first came to Vienna it was one small room and not always enough to eat.'

Megan didn't doubt his suffering but she resented his arrogance which as always was quick to surface. 'You were fortunate you had a talent, or you might still be in that situation.'

He shook his head and then sighed. 'It was my mother's hard work which saved us. You can't know anything about it.'

He put down the music once more and she said sharply, 'I'm not going to apologise for that, Gregor.'

He raised his eyes to meet hers, something which caused an involuntary flutter of her heart. 'I would be very annoyed if you did.'

'When do you intend to go to Salzburg?' she asked with sudden interest to fill an awkward silence.

He gave her a puzzled look and she went on to explain although she couldn't understand why she should need to, 'The opera you're producing for Signorina Lamarti.'

'Oh, *Lucia*,' he answered, his face clearing immediately. 'I go to Salzburg several times a week to rehearse.'

Megan's eyes opened wide, her awkwardness in his company for the moment forgotten. 'Not since we arrived, surely?'

He laughed then. 'Of course.'

'You can't possibly commute.'

82

'It's quite easy, I assure you. By air it's only a short journey, and there is a plane always available at the airport.' He have her a long, considering look which caused her to turn her attention to Stephan again. 'I am going there tomorrow. There is to be a dress rehearsal. Perhaps you would like to accompany me?'

The prospect was an attractive one. Seeing Salzburg was something she had always wanted to do.

'Does the invitation include Stephan?'

'Naturally.'

'That would be wonderful,' she told him breathlessly. 'Oh, how I envy you your talent.'

The look he gave her then was one of surprise. 'Thank you, but, you know, the world needs lawyers, too, to disentangle us from our own follies. However,' he added with a sigh, 'just now I would be much happier if you were a secretary instead.'

She looked puzzled and he shrugged in a way that was wholly Continental.

'My own secretary is ill and I have been unable to obtain a temporary replacement. The letters are piling up on my desk.'

Startled she told him, 'But I can type.' He looked disbelieving until she explained, 'It's true; when I was a student I learned to type so I could earn some money during the holidays. It's been very useful, too. Where I work we can't afford a secretary, so I type all the letters and documents myself.'

He continued to look puzzled. 'Why can't you afford a secretary?'

She laughed then at his bewilderment. 'I think you have the wrong idea of my work, Gregor. My services are free, you see . . .'

'A lawyer who doesn't get paid?'

'A much needed service, I assure you.' She looked regretful. 'I'd be glad to do your letters for you, only my knowledge of German is very limited, I'm afraid; it's certainly not nearly good enough to translate letters.'

He waved his hand in the air. 'Most

of them are in English anway. The other languages are no problem either — you'll see. Come along with me and I'll show you before you change your mind.'

He took her hand and began to draw her towards the door. 'What about Stephan?' she asked in bewilderment.

He was still struggling to perfect the nocturne, his young brow furrowed with the concentration it needed. Megan had the oddest feeling she was looking at Gregor as a child.

'Don't you worry about the boy; I shall keep him busy.'

His voice had the effect of making her start out of her thoughts and she allowed him to pull her away from the piano at last. When they reached the door he called out to the boy. 'Keep on practising, Stephan.'

The child looked exasperated. 'For how long?'

'If you work really hard, in about ten years you might be ready for the concert stage.'

Stephan's face crumpled with dismay and he swung his legs around on the piano stool to face them. 'Ten years!'

Outside, Megan, although amused, retorted, 'You shouldn't have said that to him; ten years to a child of his age is as good as for ever.'

'If he's serious about his art he mustn't have any illusions. Excellence has a very high price.'

'Well, I suppose you know all about that,' she answered grudgingly.

They crossed the hall and he opened a door which led to a small study. As she stepped inside Megan could immediately understand his concern; the desk, a large, generous antique one, was littered with letters, both opened and unopened. As she picked up one or two and gazed at them uncomprehendingly he opened one of the desk drawers and pulled out a sheaf of papers.

'These are the replies — in various languages. The English one you'll understand, naturally, but there are answers in French and German as well.

Leave all the ones you're not sure about, but these replies will cover the majority of the letters.'

Megan laughed and ran one hand through her hair. 'How do you know how to answer each one?'

'All those are fan letters.' He cast her a quick smile. 'It's quite all right, Megan. I compose the replies in the first place and sign every one, so I'm not cheating. If you have any queries I shall be in the house all afternoon, no doubt in the salon with your nephew.'

'Our nephew,' she couldn't resist reminding him and was rewarded by a smile.

He went towards the door and she immediately began to sort through the letters, which in itself seemed to be a daunting task. Suddenly becoming aware that he had paused by the door, she looked up.

'I really am grateful to you.'

Her heart felt suddenly light. The arrogance was gone and, after all, it was only a small part of what was really a very charming personality. She returned his smile, feeling glad that long ago she had decided to learn to type.

When he had gone she looked around. Not surprisingly, large tomes of music were lying all over the place. Megan collected them all together and put them on the only other piece of furniture in the room, a large sofa. As she did so she could easily imagine Gregor falling asleep on it after working so hard he was no longer able to keep fatigue at bay.

Having put the room into some semblance of order she began to divide up the letters into their respective languages. There were so many the task took her some considerable time before she could actually begin to type the replies.

Frau Hemmel interrupted once to bring her a pot of coffee and a more than generous helping of her own *apfel strudel*.

Megan viewed it longingly as she

lamented, 'Oh, Frau Hemmel, I am going to become so fat by the time I leave here!'

The nearest thing to a smile crossed the woman's face. '*Fraulein*, young women today are far too troubled by the state of their waistlines. You are much too thin to have to worry.'

Megan laughed, and when the woman had gone, she settled down to type, copying the samples Gregor had left with her. Inevitably, it was easier to type the English-language ones first. She discovered that they had come from all parts of the English-speaking world and was amazed at the devotion they expressed, something she had, up until then, associated only with pop and film stars.

As always, when hard at work, she had begun to feel she was doing very well when the ringing of the telephone at her elbow startled her. She let it ring several times before reluctantly lifting the receiver.

'*Ja? Bitte?*' she asked nervously, aware

that she was unlikely to understand the caller's reply.

'Herr Davos, *bitte*,' came the answer and Megan recognised immediately the voice of Francesca Lamarti.

Knowing that she spoke excellent English, Megan said then, 'Signorina Lamarti, this is Megan Amery.'

The woman was clearly taken aback, as the momentary silence indicated. 'So you are still in Vienna?'

'Unfortunately Gregor hasn't been able to locate Alexis.'

'How are you and the little boy?'

'We are both fine, thank you. And you?' she asked, hastily.

'As always in excellent health and spirits, *cara*.'

There was another momentary silence and Megan said quickly, 'Gregor is somewhere in the house. Shall I go and find him for you?'

'No, no; if he is not there, I will not have you trouble.'

'It's really no trouble . . . '

'I know I can rely upon you to give

him a message.'

'Of course.'

'I am due to go to Salzburg with him tomorrow morning . . . '

'Oh, yes, I know about it. In fact, Gregor has invited Stephan and me to come along, too — just for the ride.'

There was a momentary silence at the other end and then she went on, 'That is most unlike Gregor.'

'It isn't often his nephew comes to stay.'

'That might well be so, but Gregor is so involved in his work he rarely allows anyone outside it to intrude. You are very honoured, *cara*.'

Megan didn't know whether Francesca intended to be flattering or sarcastic. Before she could decide the diva went on, 'Well, perhaps you could tell him I am going to Salzburg today instead. I have an apartment there and I must make some domestic arrangements before the Festival begins. Be kind enough to tell Gregor that I will meet him at the Festival Playhouse at the time arranged.'

'Of course. I'll see he gets the message as soon as possible.'

'Thank you,' Francesca answered sweetly, 'but before tomorrow will do just as well. *Arrivederci.*'

At the other end Megan cradled the receiver thoughtfully for a moment or two before putting it down.

She recalled Stephan's question, asking his uncle if he were going to marry Francesca.

'*If only she would have me!*' he had replied and his tone had been unmistakably regretful.

Poor Gregor, she thought, staring at the now silent telephone; somehow she was able to understand quite easily how devastated he must feel at loving in vain.

6

The aeroplane which was to take them to Salzburg stood at the far side of the airport, well away from the normal commercial traffic and it was the smallest Megan had ever seen. Stephan, whilst disappointed it wasn't a big jet, was clearly delighted that only their own party, which included two singers in the opera, was to go.

Megan was not quite certain she liked to travel in so small an aircraft which seemed to be buffeted by every draught of air. However, having committed herself she kept silent and took her seat next to Stephan.

As they fastened their seatbelts, Gregor said, 'Allow me to introduce our travelling companions. Herr Trissen and Herr Moritz, members of the opera company.'

She acknowledged the introduction

and Gregor went on, looking at the younger of the two, 'Peter Moritz is to sing Edgar.'

Megan gave him a second look. He was rather handsome and he smiled roguishly. 'A journalist was recently asking me why operatic heroes always lose their women at the end. I told her I didn't know the reason why, but agreed it was most unfair.'

Megan laughed. 'How I agree with you. But it's even less fair that the heroines die.'

'Ah, yes,' he reflected sadly, 'on stage I have mourned so many lovely ladies.'

Gregor added, leaning towards her, 'In real life I can assure you Peter has done no such thing. Women are invariably left to mourn him.'

The young tenor thought this very amusing. Megan looked at the other singer who, it appeared spoke no English.

For most of the short journey Gregor was in conversation with the two members of the opera's cast, no doubt discussing their parts, and as soon as the landscape beneath them changed to the grandeur which surrounded Salzburg, Megan's attention was riveted on the green-swathed peaks and emerald lakes which nestled beneath them.

When the journey was over at last with no mishap to the tiny aeroplane, a chauffeur driven limousine was waiting at the airport to whisk them through uninspiring suburbs and then along the banks of the Salzach river through the old town which appeared to be unchanged since the time of Mozart. At last the car drew up outside the Festivalspeilhaus built especially to house Festival attractions.

Since leaving the airport Gregor seemed totally preoccupied with the task before him which did not surprise Megan. Salzburg Festival audiences were notoriously critical and any new production was watched for the slightest failing. The very thought of it caused a tremor of trepidation on his behalf.

The hall was the largest Megan had ever seen, seeming even more huge for not being packed with an audience of thousands. Members of the orchestra were already tuning up their instruments and Francesca was on the stage, bewigged and in her costume. As Gregor hurried down the aisle, her face was transformed into a welcoming smile.

'She is very beautiful,' Stephan murmured, as overwhelmed as she, it appeared.

They sat down towards the back of the auditorium so as not to cause any distraction. Gregor threw off his jacket and immediately went on stage to speak with Francesca. Then after a while he went back to the orchestra and Francesca launched into a solo aria, telling of her love for Edgar. Her voice was incredible and it filled the entire auditorium. Megan felt privileged to hear it first hand and to see the two of them at work. Gregor seemed to be able to extract the best performance from her with apparently little effort.

Megan was quite content to remain and watch the birth of what must surely become a famous partnership, but inevitably Stephan grew restless and she was certain he would not wish to remain for the entire dress rehearsal.

Reluctantly she hurried him out of the auditorium between scenes whilst Gregor was on the stage directing the company. Sadly, she realised he would not be even aware of their departure.

Once outside, however, she did feel a stirring of excitement. The town still retained its medieval intimacy and was already filling with visitors to the most prestigious music festival in the whole world. There was a definite feeling of tension in the air which was almost tangible.

'Where do you want to go?' she asked Stephan, her mind still lingering on the rehearsal they'd left.

'To the fortress,' was his unhesitating answer as he pulled her by the hand along crowded streets. 'Papa brought me here last year after we'd been boating on Trauensee. I fed some swans on the lake; they weren't a bit afraid of our boat.' He looked suddenly pensive. 'Do you think he will be coming back to Vienna soon?'

'I'm sure he must, darling. After all, it will soon be time for your regular visit anyway.'

'He's promised to take me skiing at Christmas this year. I've never been skiing before. Papa's got a lodge at Kitzbühel.'

It was high summer, but the thought of Christmas gave her a pang, for by that time she would be long back at work, dealing as always with a multitude of other people's problems. Megan could not imagine why for once the thought gave her no satisfaction.

Stephan was skipping ahead, down a narrow street which must have been unchanged since the time Mozart walked along it, probably no older than Stephan was now. Shopkeepers still hung out their wrought iron shop signs and the roofs of opposite buildings were so close together they cut out the sun.

Stephan stopped to peer into a shop window where traditional Tyrolean hats and dirndls were for sale.

'Do you think a dirndl would suit me, Stephan?' she asked, as she followed his example and peered into the window, too.

'I think it would suit Signorina Lamarti.'

'A potato sack would look good on her,' Megan replied, a mite sourly, reflecting that even a boy of Stephan's age was aware of her charisma.

Suddenly she was aware he was looking up at her with a perplexed frown on his face. 'Why was her hair a different colour?'

'It wasn't really. She was wearing a wig for her part. She's supposed to be a young woman forced into marriage to a man she doesn't love.'

'Was Mummy forced into marrying Papa?'

'Of course not!' Megan answered

laughingly. 'What gave you such a silly idea?'

He lifted his thin shoulders into a shrug. 'Mummy doesn't love him.'

Megan sighed, wondering how best to explain the situation to him. Before she could do so he said, 'I suppose Signorina Lamarti dies at the end of the opera. People are always dying in operas. That's why I don't like them.'

'It only happens in tragic operas. It wouldn't be tragic if she didn't. It never happens in comic operas. Besides, it's not really Signorina Lamarti who dies; it's the character she plays.' She took his hand and they walked on. 'She kills her husband when she realises she has lost the man she really loves and then she pretends to die. Oh, I think we're here,' she said as they walked through an old churchyard.

Although the regular funicular plied its way to and from the Hohen-Salzburg Fortress which dominated the town's skyline, Stephan insisted that they walk the seemingly countless steps to the top. Megan discovered she was not nearly as fit as she had thought as she panted her way up the steps behind her nephew. Once they had reached the top Stephan ran on ahead, inspecting the cannons and waving her on to the parapet.

The view, she discovered, once she had caught her breath, was worth the climb. From one side the wooded mountains and green valleys which stretched into Bavaria and from the other the red roofs of Salzburg itself, pierced in many places by soaring steeples from which bells rang out at regular intervals. The entire town, old and new, divided by the river, lay spread out before them and Megan drew in a deep breath of satisfaction.

Stephan explored happily, running to and fro whilst she rested against one of the ancient walls, just taking in the view and reflecting that she had not experienced so much contentment for as long as she could recall. The fact that

Gregor was a part of that feeling was a thought which came unbidden to her mind and was just as instantly dismissed.

'Aunt Meg!'

She turned on her heel as Stephan came running up to her, breathless with excitement.

'I'm starving!'

At this she burst out laughing, her pensive thoughts totally dismissed. 'I'm not surprised. It's all those steps.' She took his hand in hers. 'We'll go and find somewhere to eat, providing we go down on the funicular and not by the steps.'

He was happy enough to agree and they went in search of a suitable eating place. In summer, in Salzburg at Festival time, the town was en fête, so it wasn't difficult to find somewhere nice. It was warm enough to eat outdoors and they found a café with tables on a forecourt which overlooked one of the town's many churches.

The climb had given Megan an

appetite, too, and they lunched on soup with dumplings, boiled beef and, inevitably, Stephen enjoyed a piece of sticky sachertorte for dessert.

'I never used to like coming to Austria much,' he confided as he finished his glass of orange juice and gave the plate one last scrape with his spoon.

'Obviously you do now,' Megan answered, watching him indulgently.

He bestowed on her one of his rare smiles. 'This time I do.'

Hesitantly she asked, 'Doesn't your uncle usually see a lot of you?'

He shook his head. 'Whenever I've been here before Uncle Gregor's usually away somewhere.'

'Then we're really lucky this time,' she told him, affecting a bright voice which sounded totally alien to her own ears.

After lunch they wandered back in the general direction of the Festival Playhouse. From time to time she caught sight of posters advertising

Gregor's production of *Lucia di Lammermor*. Gregor and Francesca. The coupling of their names, even if only on posters almost seem to mock her, although Megan couldn't understand why it should seem like that.

As they came to Mozart's birthplace, hordes of visitors were making a pilgrimage and Stephan insisted upon going in, too.

'He was only my age when he played for the royal courts of Europe,' the boy said in wonder as they came out into the afternoon sunlight once again.

Megan cast him an amused look. 'Mozart was a genius, Stephan. Others, I'm afraid, just have to practise.'

He frowned as they walked in the shadow of ancient houses which looked out across the Salzach to the Mirabell Gardens at the other side.

'Do you think Uncle Gregor had to practise, too?'

'I'm certain he did.' She glanced at her watch. 'And we shall have to get back to the rehearsal. I forgot to ask what time we were supposed to be leaving for Vienna.'

'It will probably be late and I'll be able to go to bed late, too, although Uncle Gregor did say he was conducting in Vienna tonight.'

'When did he tell you that?'

'He didn't, but I heard him telling Herr Moritz when we were in the plane this morning.'

Megan looked surprised. 'Your German must be good.'

'Uncle Gregor says it's appalling.'

'I hate to think what he'd say about mine,' she answered with a laugh.

The boy looked crestfallen. 'I suppose that means we won't be going back late after all.'

Megan laughed again. 'Well, it has been a long day anyway. We're all going to be tired by the time we get back.'

They slipped into the auditorium much as they had left — unseen. It was as if they'd never left, for the players were still hard at work, and Megan was bound to wonder if they'd stopped long enough to eat.

When they arrived Gregor was once again on stage with Francesca, giving her last minute directions. After a few moments he returned to the orchestra and the scene continued. Megan watched enraptured as Francesca became the crazed Lucia, having killed her husband. Suddenly in the middle of the aria she began to cough, at first with a light delicacy and then more convulsively. As the music died away abruptly, Megan caught her breath.

Gregor said in a weary voice, 'Franzi, *liebchen*, remember you're Lucia and not Mimi.'

Someone sniggered, but having recovered from the bout of coughing Francesca let out a flow of Italian invective, gesticulating in the grandest operatic manner whilst at Megan's side Stephan began to squirm restlessly. Gregor threw down the baton and ran on to the stage taking the steps two at a time.

Megan couldn't hear what they were

saying but as Gregor put his hands on her shoulders and looked at her keenly, Francesca was shaking her head vehemently. At last he drew her into his arms and kissed her on both cheeks, something which caused Megan to look away. Moments later Gregor dismissed the orchestra and chorus and, snatching up his jacket from where he'd thrown it earlier, hurried down the aisle.

As he approached, Megan jumped to her feet. 'There's nothing wrong, is there?'

His face relaxed into a smile. 'Just a minor crisis. I'm used to them. Franzi thinks she is getting a cold.'

'But surely that's quite serious for an opera singer, isn't it?'

'It certainly puts an end to this particular rehearsal.' He glanced at his watch. 'It was going very well, but I think I've worked her too hard and we mustn't take any chances with her voice.'

'What does it mean?'

'She will just have to rest for a few

days, that's all.' He began to move on again. 'If you two will wait for me outside in the lobby I'll let the airport know we're on our way and I shall also take the precaution of telephoning Franzi's doctor in Salzburg.'

'Can't you at least go on and rehearse the rest of the company? It seems such a pity . . . '

'We've gone past the stage when that would be useful. What we must have now are full-scale rehearsals.' He touched her arm. 'Excuse me for a few minutes and I'll make those calls.'

Megan and her nephew were waiting in the lobby when he came out of the office and immediately cast her a reassuring smile. 'The plane will be ready for us when we arrive.'

'And the doctor?'

'He is going to call in to see Franzi this evening. She keeps a flat here all the year round.'

'I can understand that; it's a beautiful town.'

He gave her a long look before ushering them out to where the limousine was waiting for them. The moment they got in, Stephan began to chatter on about all they'd done that day. Megan needed to say very little although Gregor cast her a glance now and again.

The journey back to Vienna was soon completed and in an amazingly short time a car was speeding them back into the city.

'You must be exhausted,' she said when at last Stephan fell silent, beginning to droop after such a long and eventful day.

Gregor looked down at the child and his expression softened. 'He'll be all right after a night's rest.'

Megan looked up at Gregor in surprise. 'I did mean you.'

To her further surprise he laughed. 'This is nothing! Only half the day has gone for me. Tonight I'm conducting at the Musikvereinssaal.'

At the reminder she sat up straight.

'Isn't that when Signorina Lamarti was to sing, too?'

'Franzi wasn't engaged to sing, just to accompany me to the reception afterwards.' He paused, eyeing her hopefully. 'Actually, I was hoping you would be kind enough to take her place.'

She stared at him in astonishment for a moment or two. 'Me?'

He looked amused. 'Yes, you.'

'Oh, I couldn't.' She laughed. 'Apart from all other considerations, I haven't a suitable dress to wear. You did mention it was a gala evening and I know what that means in this city.'

He waved his hand in the air. 'That's no problem. You see, it was Franzi's idea and . . . '

Megan averted her gaze, murmuring, 'Oh.'

'She promised to telephone her maid here in Vienna and have her bring a gown over. She thinks you are a similar size and women usually know these things, I believe.'

Megan was almost speechless. 'I can't go to this event wearing one of her gowns. It wouldn't suit me, for one thing.'

'Why on earth not?' he asked, considerably bewildered.

'Oh, men have no notion about these things. It's bound to be a glamorous gown.'

'So?'

'I am not a glamorous person, unlike Signorina Lamarti.'

'If she is glamorous it's only because she wears that kind of gown.'

'It's bound to have cost her a fortune. I really couldn't take the responsibility. What if I spill something on it?'

He smiled, making her feel foolish for such protests which were perfectly valid to her.

'I am quite convinced you will do any gown justice, and as for all this talk of responsibility, Franzi isn't the kind of woman who would care too much about a stain, if it occurred, which I doubt.'

'I don't think you know a lot about women, Gregor.'

'You are probably quite right about that.' He peered at her earnestly. 'I suppose I am asking too much of you after all else you've done.'

She shook her head, gasping, 'I won't pretend it wouldn't be marvellous, but surely there are others more suited . . . '

'No, it's settled. You will go.'

The car drew up outside the house. Megan's head was still in a whirl. Francesca had to be very certain of his affections to suggest another woman take her place and even provide the clothes. Even as a stand-in she couldn't deny the attraction of his proposition. It would be a unique opportunity to enjoy a gala concert as only the Viennese could stage.

Whilst her mind grappled with thoughts about the concert, Gregor got out of the car and lifted out Stephan who had fallen asleep on the seat between them.

When they reached the front door he said, 'Time is a little short, I'm afraid. I'll ask Frau Hemmel to bring you something to eat in your room while you're getting ready.'

'Oh, please don't bother!' she gasped. 'I'm far too excited to eat anything at all!'

Her enthusiasm caused him to smile again, making her feel a little foolish.

'Good. Save your appetite for later, for the President's reception!'

7

A strange woman was in Megan's room when she returned to it after settling Stephan in his bed, fortunately somewhat earlier than usual because of the long and tiring day.

'I am Signorina Lamarti's maid,' the woman announced in German, and Megan's startled eyes immediately went to the bed where a ball gown had been laid out.

She hurried across the room to look at it more closely, for she had never seen such a lovely gown, even though she had been prepared for something special. The skirt was made up of yards of white tulle and the bodice which left one shoulder bare was of silver lace. A matching shawl of silver lace was laid next to it.

'Signorina Lamarti has asked that I help you dress,' the woman told her as she gazed at the gown.

Megan gave her her attention at last. 'Oh, that is very kind of her, but I can manage.'

'Perhaps I can arrange your hair for you, *fraulein*.'

Megan ran her hands through her unruly locks and was at least glad of that, but once she was dressed she was amazed at her own appearance. In the shimmering gown and with her hair swept up off her shoulders and into a sophisticated style, she scarcely recognised her own reflection in the mirror.

It was with some hesitation that she finally left the room after thanking Francesca's maid, Helga, for her invaluable help. She approached the salon experiencing a great feeling of shyness. As it happened she was given a respite, for Gregor was talking to someone on the telephone.

He was half turned away from her, but her heart gave a little leap at how handsome he looked in white tie and tails. Her hands were unsteady as they gripped the silver evening bag which Helga had thoughtfully included.

After a few minutes he put down the receiver, but he was still unaware of her presence. For a moment she was alarmed, for he appeared to be stricken, his face almost ashen.

'Gregor, is anything wrong?' she asked hesitantly.

He stood up straight then and turned around to face her. 'No!' He smiled and she immediately felt relieved. 'You look quite splendid. The gown looks as if it was made for you.'

She knew her cheeks were flooding with colour, but she could do nothing about it as he came towards her.

'Signorina Lamarti must have sent me her best gown. I feel quite guilty.'

'She has dozens, so you needn't worry.' He took her arm and led her towards the stairs. 'The car is already here; we had better hurry. It wouldn't do to be late.'

As they got in she said pensively, 'I

can't help feeling guilty over this, Gregor; if Signorina Lamarti hadn't taken ill . . . '

He gave her a wry look as the car set off. 'I don't believe for one moment that Franzi is really ill. She is probably tired and couldn't be bothered with yet another reception.'

'Another! Well, it's not likely that I'll attend any more, but if I do I hope I never get so blasé about it.'

'Ah, but just imagine if it were happening all the time,' he pointed out.

'I still don't believe I would ever grow tired of it.'

Throughout the short journey to the concert hall he stared out of the window as if deep in thought. It seemed he had forgotten she was even there.

She thought it was probable he was always like that before a concert but more likely he was thinking about the beautiful soprano with whom he would rather be. However, even with that thought in her mind she was determined not to allow the knowledge to detract from her enjoyment that evening.

★ ★ ★

The flower-bedecked Musikvereinssaal was already packed with people when Megan took her seat. She gazed about her in awe, for all were handsomely dressed as herself and the silver lace gown was in no way out of place. Jewels glittered beneath the lights of the auditorium and as always on such an occasion there was an excitement in the air which had already communicated itself to her.

Gradually the musicians took their places and began to tune up, causing her to grow more uneasy. After what seemed to be an age Gregor made his entrance and was given a huge ovation by the audience. Megan wondered if he was nervous, too, for she found that her own palms were damp.

The clapping died away at last and Gregor raised his baton. The hall filled with the first strains of music and it was then that Megan wondered why she had been so nervous on his behalf. He extracted the most marvellous response from the orchestra as the strains of first Schoenberg and then Bruckner filled the vast concert hall.

During the interval she went backstage but there were so many people milling about she was forced to return to her seat before she found him. All too soon the last magnificent strains of Mahler's Fifth Symphony died away to tumultuous applause. No one applauded more enthusiastically than Megan who was glad to see Gregor flushed with the triumph of the evening. She was sure he was used to such adulation by now, but he couldn't possibly view it with cynicism.

It was a long time before he was allowed to leave the podium but when he did she went once more backstage, this time to find him surrounded by people who wished to congratulate him personally.

At last he caught sight of her and immediately excused himself from the throng of admirers.

'Oh, that was marvellous!' she enthused, certain that he had heard that praise many times already.

'It is a great orchestra,' was his generous response and then, taking her arm and guiding her to the stage door, he said, 'Let's not keep the best part of the evening and the country's President waiting.'

'It's the conductor who makes an orchestra truly great,' she told him as he hurried her out to where a car was again waiting for them.

More admirers were waiting by the stage door, too, and he paused to sign some autographs and exchange a few words with them.

As they got into the car Megan heard one of them say, 'I wonder who *she* is?'

She smiled to herself and didn't doubt that they'd be disappointed if they knew.

As the car sped away into the night

towards the Belvedere Palace, she turned to him and said, 'One thing is puzzling me; where was your music? I didn't see any at all during the concert.'

He had seemed distant again and looked at her blankly for a moment or two before answering, 'Whenever I can, I conduct from memory. That way I can give all my attention to the orchestra.'

She was yet again astounded. 'That's incredible. It must be a unique feat, Gregor.'

She detected a faint smile in the darkness. 'I don't think so.'

She didn't trouble to argue with him. The car drove through the gates of the Belvedere. At the main entrance a liveried footman was waiting to open the car door and other footmen lined the staircase leading to the main reception room.

What followed their arrival seemed like a dream to Megan. The place was already teeming with people, most of whom who had been at the concert, and everyone was in splendid attire.

Megan was introduced to so many of them she couldn't hope to remember them, except for the President of Austria, of course. That experience wouldn't fade quickly from her mind. Some people conversed with her in English but others spoke only German. Nevertheless she enjoyed meeting them all whilst the orchestra played in the background, inevitably Strauss waltzes.

For most of the evening they were so occupied there was little time for dancing but Gregor did manage to get away from all those who wished to speak with him and waltzed her around the floor. Megan melted into his arms quite naturally and wished that the evening might never end.

Champagne flowed as if from the fountains in the grounds of the palace and the supper, in the form of a buffet, was more like a banquet. Gregor now did justice to the food — it appeared he had not eaten since breakfast — but Megan was far too excited to do anything except pick at her plateful of delicious morsels.

'I shall remember tonight for all my life,' she told him.

He looked up from his plate. His expression was that of an adult indulging a child, but she didn't mind it.

'So shall I, Megan, I assure you.'

She cast him a considering look. Of course he would. He'd remember it as the night Francesca Lamarti left him with only a dull English solicitor to escort to an important reception.

'You lead a very busy life . . . ' she ventured, wondering why she had known so little of him before.

The answer to that was quite simple, she realised a moment later. Vivien talked only about herself and no one else intruded. It would not occur to her to mention that her brother-in-law was a world famous conductor.

He laughed unexpectedly. 'Megan, this is the summer; it is my quietest time.'

She wasn't sure whether he was

joking or not. A constant stream of people clamoured to speak with him, or just shake his hand which made conversation between him and Megan a little difficult.

After supper, finding herself separated from him she wandered out on to the terrace where the air was fresher and from which she could view the lights which played on the dancing fountains, and the illuminated buildings of Vienna which spread out beyond the gardens like a jewelled scarf.

Megan lost count of how long she was out there just enjoying the quiet and the view. The sound of the orchestra came to her faintly on the breeze but did not intrude. Fleetingly she wondered if Vivien had got the contract she was seeking and thought, just at that moment, she wouldn't change places with anyone else in the world, but she didn't examine too closely the reason for her sudden change of heart.

A step on the terrace behind her

made her look round and her heart gave another one of those leaps when she saw it was Gregor.

'Ah, so here you are. For a while I was afraid I'd lost you for good. I'm sorry we were parted.'

He was looking at her anxiously and her face relaxed into a smile. 'That's all right. I understand that you're very much in demand, and rightly so.'

'As long as you're not bored. It's hard for you not knowing anyone and not being able to speak the language.'

'It really doesn't matter. It's amazing how people can always make themselves understood.'

'Yes, I've noticed,' he answered, coming towards her at last. 'The air is much better out here.'

As if to illustrate it, Megan took a deep breath. 'It's lovely and I'm enjoying the view.'

'It is marvellous, isn't it? It sometimes takes a visitor to remind residents what a jewel we have in this city.'

'Who does the palace belong to?'

He turned on his heel to give her his attention. 'It belongs to the country now to be used for official functions such as this one. It was built, though, by Prince Eugene of Savoy. He was a professional soldier who fought for Austria and was rewarded by the Emperor with this land on which he built the palace.'

'He had very good taste.'

'Which is more than can be said about the relative who inherited this place. She never lived here and never cared for it. She just sold the furniture and left the place empty.'

'So he was never married?'

His eyes sparkled. 'Fighting wars was a demanding career but I believe whenever he was in residence he was never lonely. Most of the beautiful women of Vienna came here at some time or another.'

'He sounds rather like you,' she said pertly.

'Oh no, not quite.'

She laughed softly. 'Well, I do know

you're not a soldier.'

'And I have been married.'

Her smile faded. She stared at him in astonishment and began to stammer, 'I didn't know ... I am sorry, Gregor ... really ... '

He put one hand over hers where it rested on a balustrade. 'Don't apologise. It's no secret and it doesn't matter any more.'

'You're divorced?' she asked hesitantly.

'We would have been, I dare say, only she died before it could be arranged.'

She kept on looking at him but his face betrayed no emotion. 'I really am very sorry, Gregor.'

'It was a long time ago,' he answered with a sigh, lifting his hand from hers and walking away from her along the terrace. 'It started out well. We were both students at the Academy of Music, too young and idealistic to know what we were getting into, but at the time we weren't aware of that. I think I felt the need to make a real home for Alexis. Our mother was dead by then and he was still quite young. It wasn't a very good reason to get married. Anyway, when I began to travel a lot with my work there began to be friction between us. I did neglect her, I admit. One day she left a note to say she had met someone else; a ski instructor from one of the resorts. Not long afterwards I heard she'd been killed in an avalanche.'

'How awful! I am sorry.'

'As I said, it was a long time ago. I only remember occasionally. In fact, when I do think about it I can hardly believe it was me.'

She continued to gaze at him worriedly. 'You didn't really neglect her, not in the real sense. You're blaming yourself unjustly.'

Her words made him smile. 'You're very kind, but don't worry; it hasn't blighted my life.'

Feeling foolish at her defence of him she turned away, her cheeks growing hot despite the coolness of the night breeze. As far as the horizon, lights winked and twinkled in the darkness.

'She should have understood; you are not an ordinary man and she was a musician, too.'

'She was a woman.'

'A talent such as yours must always come first,' she said, more fiercely than she intended.

He looked at her with interest. 'In her place would you have felt any differently? You have already said your own career is the most important thing to you.'

Megan averted her eyes in confusion. 'In that case I can't really condemn her, can I? I can't say how I would behave because I've never been in that situation.'

He walked away from her again. 'Megan, I am faced with a particular situation just now and I don't know what to do about it.'

She looked up again, her heart beating unaccountably fast. He turned abruptly on his heel to face her once again and his expression was grim.

'What on earth is it?' she asked.

'That telephone call you mentioned, when you came in earlier. It was a last-minute invitation to conduct a concert in Budapest. The original conductor has been taken ill.'

She stared at him for a moment or two without comprehending and then she cried, 'Budapest! But you . . . '

'Yes, I was born there, but I haven't been back since nineteen fifty-six. I was a child then.'

She took a step towards him. 'But if you want to go back now, can you? I mean . . . '

'Yes, I know exactly what you mean. I am now a citizen of Austria. Besides, the country is run differently now. There's no reason why I can't go back — if I wish.'

'And that's the real dilemma?'

He nodded and she asked, 'When is it?'

'The day after tomorrow.'

'So soon. Do you have the time to spare?'

He shrugged. 'I doubt if Franzi will be fit enough to rehearse by that time, so by chance I am free to do the concert.'

'So the decision is purely on personal grounds,' she mused. 'I suppose you have a great many painful memories of how it was.'

'They are very ugly.'

She knew as he spoke he was remembering and very gently she asked, 'Do you have any relatives left in Hungary?'

He drew a sigh. 'Not as far as I know. My father died early in the uprising and as far as I am aware so did my elder brother.'

Her heart filled with pain for him. 'Oh, Gregor, I had no idea you had another brother. Are you certain he's dead?'

'No, I can't be certain of anything, but it's likely. He was only fifteen at the time. When we were about to leave my mother pleaded with him to come with us but he insisted he would stay on and fight for Hungary. We never saw him or heard from him again. My mother died with his name on her lips.'

'But there is no actual proof that he's dead?'

'So many nameless ones died. Who would have known his name in all that chaos? Over the years I've made enquiries only to meet silence. Emil must be dead.'

After a moment she said, 'Gregor, I think you should go back. Your memories are understandably bitter but perhaps that pain can be eased by seeing the country actually at peace again.'

He looked at her for a long moment before saying, 'You're correct, of course. Now I've been invited it's an excellent opportunity to go, but it isn't an easy decision.'

'I don't think you'll regret it.'

'Will you come with me?'

Although she no longer thought of

her stay in relation to Alexis' absence, she was nevertheless taken aback and she began to make an excuse, but he took her hands in his again.

'Please, Megan. I would like you to come.'

She looked up at him then, her cheeks growing pink with pleasure. 'If you don't mind my bringing a small boy along, too.'

'If it were not for that small boy you would not be here now,' he pointed out. 'It has been fortunate for both of us that circumstances connived at your staying. I only wish you would agree to stay on even longer.'

Confused she answered, 'Once Alexis is back in Vienna there will be no need for me to stay.'

'You make a very good secretary. I would gladly employ you on a permanent basis.'

The notion made her laugh but he was looking at her seriously. 'That was a foolish thing to say; an insulting one.'

She shrugged. 'You complimented me.'

'You have a more important career in London.'

She withdrew her hands from his, murmuring, 'I always thought so before.'

The shawl had slipped from her shoulders and she shivered in the sudden breeze. He immediately draped it around her shoulders again and it seemed that his hands lingered there for longer than was necessary. Megan stiffened, her entire body tense at the touch of his fingers, and then his hands dropped to his sides.

'You look tired, *liebchen*. I think we will be forgiven for leaving now, don't you?'

She smiled uncertainly, suddenly unable to speak. Instead she nodded and followed him back inside.

8

He was tense; Megan could sense it as the plane began its descent for Budapest. Gregor had hardly spoken since the plane had taken off even though Stephan had scarcely stopped.

'Budapest. I've never been there before. Won't Papa be surprised when I tell him? He was born there, you know.'

Megan cast him a fond smile, although her thoughts were with Gregor. 'Won't you have a lot to tell your schoolfriends, too, at the end of the holiday?'

'I'd rather stay in Vienna with you and Uncle Gregor.'

Her smile faded. That prospect, impossible as it was, looked attractive to her, too.

'You know you have to go back to school in September. I have to return to my job long before that, and Uncle

Gregor is too busy to have you under his feet all the time.'

Gregor gave her a long look as Stephan went on, 'Every plane we've been in has been different. Did you know that? I've begun to make a note of them in one of my books.'

'My goodness! When I was your age boys collected train numbers. How times have changed.'

Gregor's tension communicated itself to her as they left the plane. It came as a relief when their passports were given no more than the usual scrutiny and with no further delay they went out to find an official car had been sent to take them to their hotel.

It was Megan's first experience of travelling with a VIP and she found it a pleasant one. The hotel was ultra-modern and she and Stephan shared a suite of communicating rooms which were both bright and spacious. She and Stephan were admiring the view from the balcony when they heard a knock on the door. As Megan turned around

Gregor came into the room, carrying an armful of letters.

'More fan mail,' Megan said delightedly as she came back into the room. 'Will you take charge of them?'

'Of course; I'm only sorry I'm not able to answer them for you. I'm sure the language would be beyond my scope.'

'I shall have to compose an answer in Hungarian,' he agreed and she gave him a concerned look. 'It's a long time since I've used my native tongue. Other languages come to me more easily these days.'

'Oh, please don't worry,' she begged, hating the way he was trying to treat this visit as just another engagement. It wasn't and no one was more aware of that fact than Megan.

His bright pretence faded then. 'I can't help myself; I've conducted most of the great orchestras of the world in front of some of the most critical audiences, but this concert is very special.'

'I know,' she answered softly, 'but it must be a great consolation to you to see how things have changed since the time you left Budapest.'

His manner brightened immediately. 'From what I've already seen, life has improved dramatically from how I remember it.'

'I'm surprised at how prosperous everyone appears. And the traffic!'

'Uncle Gregor,' Stephan called from the balcony. 'Come and see our view!'

Megan followed him on to the balcony. 'We've been treated quite royally,' he said, glancing at her.

'It's no more than is due to you,' she told him.

The hotel was situated in Pest on the banks of the Danube which swept through the city and was far from blue, at least at that moment. Gregor stood on the balcony, his hands on the balustrade, gazing across the river to Buda on the far shore. The sun was shining on the spire of St. Matthias's church and glinted off the cupola of the

#351 Sat Aug 23 2003 12:21PM
Item(s) checked out to PITRE, SHARON ANN

TITLE: Man of music [large print] / Bren
BARCODE: 32345026245770
DUE DATE: Sep 06 2003

   To renew: 596-7955
   or www.tulsalibrary.org

old Royal Palace.

'It's so beautiful,' he murmured, 'more so than I remember it.'

'Yes, it is lovely. I'm so glad.'

He looked down at her and smiled. 'So am I.'

He moved back into the sitting room. 'I must go along to the concert hall. Why don't you and Stephan order some lunch and then go out and look around for a while? I might not be back until quite late.'

With a quick wave of his hand he was gone and Megan smiled as she turned back to Stephan. 'It looks as though we're on our own again. Shall we get some lunch?'

'Only if I can have *gulyas*.'

'You can have what you like,' she told him, her mood bland, 'and if you know what you're eating, so much the better. In fact I shall join you if you can recommend *gulyas*.'

'It's something I often have when I go out with Papa. There's a restaurant in Vienna where we go sometimes; Papa knows the owner. He's from Hungary, too.' He laughed. 'We're hungry in Hungary. Hurrah!'

Megan laughed, too, and held out her hand to him. 'Come along. This place is a part of you, Stephan, so let's make the most of our time here.'

★   ★   ★

Dusk had enshrouded the Danube as Megan tucked the bedclothes around the almost sleeping child and then she tip-toed out of the bedroom and into the adjoining sitting room. She closed the door carefully and then turned on her heel, starting slightly when she realised she wasn't alone.

Gregor was sitting in one of the deep easy chairs, staring across the room and out of the window to the floodlit heights of Buda.

Megan always felt she needed to prepare herself to face him with equilibrium and was taken aback by so sudden a confrontation.

140

'I didn't know you'd come back,' she said, hesitating by the door for a moment and then, when he started to get up, she urged, 'Please don't,' and approached him at last. 'Did everything go well?'

At first glance she had seen he was still ill-at-ease and she could understand the unsettling effect this visit was having on him. In this instance pain and pleasure were too closely allied.

'Yes, it went very well. Of course, I already knew the orchestra was a good one. Fortunately, the players are very responsive and I think they're particularly pleased to have me conduct them.'

'Are you surprised?'

He smiled faintly and she sat down facing him.

'Do you know where I've been?'

'To the concert hall,' she answered in some surprise.

'Before I came back here I asked the driver to take me down the full length of Lenin Korut.'

She looked at him with interest. 'Why

did you do that?'

'Because I used to live there. I still recall the address and I couldn't resist going.'

She became suddenly tense. His moods had begun to affect her more than she believed possible.

'And?'

'The driver wasn't too keen; he has his orders, no doubt, to drive me from here to the concert hall and back again, but I managed to persuade him.'

'Is it still there?'

'Oh, yes, and amazingly our apartment looked just the same from the outside. It was on the second floor. Once, before the last war, it had been a luxury villa and afterwards it was divided into apartments for several families. It was small and cramped for five of us, but we were fortunate to have it all the same. My father had a good job and our home was better than most. Now, I suppose, another family lives there much as we did.'

'Did it hurt you to see it?' she asked anxiously.

His eyes held hers. 'Not at all. I was glad to see such normality. Nothing ever lasts, which in this case is reassuring.'

'Good things last,' she told him.

Realising this pilgrimage was absolutely necessary and of a healing nature, Megan relaxed considerably.

'The driver must have thought you were mad going to look at an ordinary house!'

'I think he was very relieved when I told him to bring me back to the hotel!' Then he asked, 'What have you and Stephan been doing?'

'We've been indulging in a little sightseeing. I took Stephan on a Danube steamer. He liked that. He's absolutely worn out now but I'm sure he's never enjoyed himself more.'

He smiled across at her. 'That is also true of me.'

Disturbed by his probing gaze, discomforted by his admission, she wondered what he would say if she told him she had fallen in love with him. The knowledge, admitted now, had been slow to come to her but the realisation was a shock and if he were to learn of it, it would spoil their new-found rapport, of that she was certain and Megan treasured it too much to do anything so foolish. When she eventually returned home she would be able to treasure, in the time to come, memories of a look, a smile, a complimentary word.

She cast him a shy look. 'We've both probably fallen into the habit of working so hard we've nearly forgotten how good it is to relax and enjoy something entirely different.'

'Well, if that is so I must thank you for helping me to remember.'

Just at that moment Megan almost wished they were back to how they were at first; uneasy allies, hardly seeing one another. It was not always easy being so close and still hiding what she had come to feel for him.

She got to her feet, saying breathlessly, 'Shall I order something to eat for you? It is growing rather late.'

He stood up then, too. 'No, thank you. I never eat before a performance, but you are quite correct about the time; I shall have to go back to my suite and change. Will you be able to leave Stephan tonight?'

'The hotel housekeeper has agreed to look in on him at frequent intervals. He doesn't usually wake up but I'll feel better if she's around — just in case.'

He gave her a thoughtful look. 'I wonder if Vivien is as concerned about him as you are?'

'I'm sure she is, Gregor. She knows he's in good hands or she wouldn't have gone away.'

He began to walk towards the door but then he paused. 'What exactly is she doing in the United States?'

'Trying for a part in an important film.'

'Who says it's important?'

Megan shrugged. 'Vivien.'

'What is important to her is perhaps not so important to anyone else.'

Her eyes narrowed. 'You don't like Vivien very much, do you?'

'I have no feeling for her of any kind.' He pushed his hands into his pockets and then brought out a letter. He smiled sheepishly as he waved it at her. 'No doubt this is from another music-lover. The doorkeeper at the concert hall handed it to me just as I was leaving and I forgot all about it until now.'

'You really should read some of those letters,' Megan told him. 'Some of those I read the other day were so nice. It's as if you were acquainted. You have friends all over the world.'

'It's a sobering thought and yet a warming feeling. Sometimes I really think that music is the universal language which everyone can understand. It unites us all, and' he added wryly, 'I do read all of them when I have the time. They mean a lot to me. Where would I be without them?'

He opened the envelope and drew out a single sheet of paper. After a moment his expression changed. Slowly, as if walking in his sleep he came back to the chair and sat down, the paper limp in his hand.

Megan was immediately concerned at the change in him. 'Gregor, what is it? What's the matter?'

'The letter . . . it's from my brother. At least that's what it says. It's signed Emil . . . '

Megan then snatched up the sheet, but she could decipher only the name at the bottom of the few lines of writing.

'Do you think it's genuine?' she asked anxiously.

He looked bewildered. 'I don't know. He doesn't say a great deal, except that he will be at the Fisherman's Bastion on Castle Hill at eleven o'clock tomorrow morning if I want to see him. *If.* As if there is any question.' He got up again, moving towards the door, still looking stunned. 'Megan, this changes everything. We shall have to stay a little while longer. Will you cancel our flight for the morning?'

She nodded her head vigorously whilst her mind still mulled over the consequences of that letter. 'Yes, yes, if that's what you want.'

Then, as he was about to leave the room, she rushed up to him and caught his arm. 'Gregor, I know what this must mean to you, but just wait and think about it for a moment before rushing into anything.'

His face reflected the bewilderment he must have been feeling. 'I cannot just ignore it, Megan.'

'That's the problem. It's obvious you'd react in this way, but how do you know this note is genuine? You've no idea how the authorities here really feel about you and it might be some elaborate plot to discredit you.'

He put one hand over hers. 'I am aware of that, but I must go if there is the slightest chance it is Emil.'

Megan knew it, of course, and she

stepped back, smiling slightly. 'I'll ring through immediately and get our flight changed for a later one.'

She stared at the door for ages after he had gone before drawing a sigh and going to the telephone. Being so sensitive to his feelings, it mattered to her almost as much as to him that the message was genuine. His happiness was paramount now and the coming concert was no longer the most exciting prospect on the horizon.

★ ★ ★

'I thought we were going back to Vienna this morning,' Stephan protested as Megan pushed the last piece of clothing into his case.

'Your uncle decided he wanted to stay a little while longer.'

'Why? Does he have another concert? I thought he only had one. Can I go this time? Please, Aunt Meg!'

She cast him a quick smile even though her thoughts were on the coming meeting. 'No, he isn't conducting another concert just now, but if he was, you are still too young to go. You'd be asleep before the interval and I'm afraid snoring just disturbs the musicians.'

The boy laughed and Megan glanced at her watch, wondering if Gregor had left for the meeting yet. Fortunately, whatever his inner feelings on the matter his performance on the previous evening had not been affected. The concert had been no less than a triumph and the Hungarian audience gave him an ovation which made it quite clear they welcomed back one of their sons. The experience was sufficient to move Megan to tears.

Gregor had seemed totally drained on their way back to the hotel. Aware he put so much of himself into his work and that thoughts of tomorrow's meeting must be in the forefront of his mind, Megan longed to take him into her arms and hold him close, but it was not for her to do so. Even when he paused outside her suite to bid her goodnight and kiss her hand, it was done almost absentmindedly.

Alone, inside the suite, she knew that sleep was a long way away and she spent some time on the balcony, gazing out across the Danube to Buda, to the Fisherman's Bastion where the meeting was to take place the next day. And much later, as she prepared for bed, Megan knew that exhausted though he may be, he would not find sleep easy to come by.

She was still with Stephan in the bedroom when she heard the door open. When she went into the adjoining room, expecting to find a chamber maid there, she was surprised to see Gregor himself.

'I thought you might have gone by now,' she greeted him uncertainly.

As she spoke she searched his face anxiously for the tell-tale signs of stress but was relieved to see him looking so refreshed and relaxed. Caring so deeply for another person was something to which she had become unaccustomed. Life's agonies were two-fold but, she supposed, so were the delights.

How different he looked in the light of day, dressed casually in jeans and a sweater, in direct contrast to the night when he was stiff and correct in white tie and tails.

'Without you and Stephan?' he answered in some surprise.

Her anxiety melted and her face softened into a smile. 'You'd best go on your own, Gregor. It's for the best.'

'But you will give me courage. Don't you realise that? I need you with me. You must come.'

Her thoughts were so chaotic she could only nod her assent. His need of her was so poignant it tore at her heart, but it also filled her with a lingering sadness, for he truly needed no one and her role at his side was a strictly temporary one. Megan knew it was just because she happened to be there. In other circumstances it might have been Francesca Lamarti, or any of the other

152

women he undoubtedly kept with him in the singer's absence.

Gregor went back towards the door. 'I think we should be leaving now. The car is waiting but the driver is somewhat puzzled as he had his orders to drive us to the airport. I told him I wanted to do some sightseeing before I go back to Vienna. I think that's reasonable enough, don't you?'

'I do,' she answered, 'but does he? Will he take us where we want to go?'

'He isn't too happy about the departure from the planned itinerary, but he will do as I ask. How can he refuse? It's one of the advantages of being a famous personality.'

She called Stephan who had been playing happily with a toy she'd bought him in the hotel shop. He came running, carrying the toy plane and immediately launched into an excited description of their ride the previous day on the Danube, viewing all the city's famous buildings from that vantage point.

Gregor listened with interest as the car sped them through the modern business heart of Pest, across the Chain Bridge to the old part of the city on wooded Castle Hill. The car sped through the narrow, winding streets to halt outside the great Gothic bulk of St. Matthias' Church which they had already seen from the hotel balcony.

Gregor told the driver to wait whilst they wandered around, at the same time glancing around him anxiously.

Megan said, feeling a little uneasy, 'Shall we wait here until you come back?'

'No,' he answered, taking hold of her arm in a firm grip.

He glanced at his watch as they walked to the ramparts of the Fisherman's Bastion. Stephan ran ahead, flying his plane aloft. The sun was shining and Megan knew they looked just like an ordinary tourist family. Her heart grew heavy as she looked up at him. If only that was what they really were, she thought. She, Gregor and

Stephan together. It would be perfect. But soon she must hand Stephan back to his real father and she would leave Gregor for ever. In a month he probably wouldn't even remember her name. Megan could scarcely bear the thought, but it wouldn't go away.

'It isn't so serious.'

His mocking voice broke into her thoughts, the seriousness of which must have been apparent to him, but for the wrong reason, of course.

Despite that she cried, 'How can you say so?'

'I shall be disappointed if it is a hoax after all, but I've been disappointed before.'

She smiled uncertainly in the face of his gentle mockery as they reached the rampart wall. All of Pest, the Danube and the green mass of St. Margaret Island was spread below them.

Stephan came rushing up to them, saying breathlessly, 'I can see our hotel from here! Can you see it?'

'Yes, and I can see the Parliament

building,' Gregor pointed out. 'There it is, on the far side of the river, just like yours is in London.'

Stephan rushed off again. Normally Megan would have spent a great deal of time enjoying the panoramic view from the Bastion, but she immediately turned her back on it and joined Gregor in looking around. For once the people strolling along the Promenade were of more interest than anything else. There were a great many people around, too, strolling in the sunshine, but none of them seemed likely to be the long-lost Emil.

After a moment Gregor seemed to relax as he leaned back against the balustrade. 'This city used to be called the Paris of the East years ago.'

'I think it has regained a great deal of its gaiety, don't you?'

He smiled down at her as she watched him anxiously. 'Yes. It has been a nice surprise.'

'Would you like to come back here to live?'

He shook his head. 'My home is in Vienna now. It is what I've known as home for the greater part of my life and my work takes me all over the civilised world.'

'Will you come back even . . . even if . . . '

'Even if I don't find Emil?' He voiced the question she dare not ask. 'Yes, I shall return. I have already received an invitation to conduct a series of concerts in the autumn.'

'That's wonderful!'

'No, it isn't,' he answered with a laugh. 'I am already committed elsewhere for all of this year and most of next, but I will come back as soon as I can.'

She cast him a curious look then. 'Then the memories *are* fading?'

He shook his head again. 'I was a child and memories linger more when they're formed in the mind of a child.' He gazed across to where Stephan was playing. 'The sound of tanks rumbling down the street, mortars going off, the cries of the dying and the wounded, will never fade entirely, but it's marvellous to see the city back to something of its old glory.'

'Do you think,' she asked timorously, 'you would recognise your brother after all these years?'

He drew a sigh. 'That's something which has been plaguing me ever since I got that letter, but I do believe I would know him.'

She looked around again. Stephan was still running to and fro with his plane held aloft, and she smiled at the sight of him playing so happily, but her smile faded somewhat as her eyes continued to rake the promenade for someone who might possibly be Emil Davos. Two men had been walking behind them when they left the car. They were now standing a few yards away, apparently enjoying the view like everyone else.

As Gregor glanced yet again at his watch, Megan said, 'There are two men standing behind us, and I'm sure they're following us, Gregor. Is it possible? Or is my imagination running amok?'

He didn't trouble even to look. 'They are watching us. They've been following me since I arrived, or at least two men just like them. I suppose it's natural to want to know exactly what I'm doing.'

She drew back a little. 'Oh, no!'

He gave her a quick glance. 'Why don't we give them something interesting to see?'

To her alarm and surprise he put his arms around her, drawing her close. His hands felt cool through the thin silk of her dress. For a long moment he looked down into her eyes before kissing her with a relentless passion she never dreamed might be hers. A pretence it might be, but Megan's response was intuitive and immediate. Her arms went round his neck and it seemed as if she had lived only for this moment.

To be held by him was all she had desired of late and in the deep recesses of her heart she knew it was all she was likely to have. One kiss to last a lifetime.

At last he let her go as Stephan came running up to them, but his eyes held hers for a moment longer.

'How I wish this plane would fly on its own like a real one!'

'I'll buy you one when we get back to Vienna,' his uncle promised, and Megan noted that his voice was harsh.

Unable to face either of them Megan turned away. The two men were in conversation and apparently unaware of all else.

Incongruously, she wondered if her lipstick were smeared, an odd thought when her emotions were in such an upheaval. A kiss to awaken a passionate response, and yet, for him, it had been only a sign of bravado. How she longed for him to speak a word of love to make it mean something more than just that.

Suddenly, she was aware that he had become tense. She looked around again to see him move away from her side. Another man was coming towards them from the direction of the church.

Megan hardly dared look, but forced herself to do so. The man was as tall as Gregor, his hair only a shade or two darker, but unlike Gregor's, his was speckled with grey. He approached hesitantly, looking anxiously across at them and Megan felt her own tension return.

Without a word to either of them, Gregor walked away, towards the man who Megan felt instinctively must be his brother. A hoax would be too cruel and she really couldn't think why one should be perpetrated.

'Where is Uncle Gregor going?' Stephan asked in a loud-voice.

'Hush,' she urged, turning away. 'He has to see someone for a little while. We'll just wait here until he returns.'

It might have been one of the most important moments of Gregor's life, but Megan's mind was still in a whirl, still tasting the saltiness of his lips on hers, the satisfaction of it tempered by her anxiety that this stranger should, after all, be Emil Davos.

To divert her own mind and Stephan's attention, she began to point out landmarks to him and the boats which were plying along the Danube until a footstep behind her caused her to swing round abruptly on her heel.

Gregor was staring at her. The man who had come to meet him could no longer be seen anywhere. Her heart began to beat loudly with an unspeakable dread.

At last he said, 'There's no doubt; he was Emil.'

Megan let out a cry of delight and hugged him excitedly. 'I'm so glad. Did he recognise you?'

'We knew each other immediately.'

Recalling the two men who'd been watching them she pulled away, looking round anxiously. 'Will there be any trouble?'

'Emil says not. Life is quite easy here now, although it has been difficult in the past.'

He took her arm and caught hold of Stephan's hand before he began to lead them back to where the car was waiting.

'Where are we going now?' she asked, laughing with sheer relief.

'I am going to buy you both the best lunch in Budapest, and then when we've celebrated I'll tell you all about it.'

'But what about our flight this afternoon?' she protested.

'Cancel it. We're going to celebrate tonight, too.' He glanced back at the two men who were also making their way towards the car. 'Come along before they have an excuse to arrest us for loitering!'

9

He was true to his word and afterwards back at the hotel, having consumed between them the bottle of champagne he'd insisted on ordering with their meal, Megan thought he looked happier and more relaxed than ever before.

'Just imagine, Megan,' he told her, sinking down into one of the armchairs in the sitting room of her suite, 'All those years he believed us to be dead, too.'

'How did he find out you weren't?' she asked, almost as excited as he.

'From the announcement on the radio about the concert. He knew immediately it must be me. I was always so passionate about music even as a small child and the coincidence would have been too great.'

'All these years he's been here in

Budapest and you didn't know. What a pity, Gregor.'

For a moment his eyes clouded. 'No, he hasn't always been here. He was in prison for years after the uprising, but,' he added, brightening, 'fortunately life hasn't been too bad for him since then. He has an apartment not too far from where we used to live, and a good job as a translator with one of the ministries.'

'Does he have any family?'

'A wife and three teenaged children. I find that very hard to imagine. Naturally, he has changed a great deal. I remember him as being full of fire, wanting to change the world. I was, I confess the one who cared only for music. He was very interested in Stephan, naturally. Alexis was a very small child himself when we left Hungary. Emil thought you were my wife at first.'

Megan looked away in confusion and then a moment later asked, 'When are you to meet again?'

'Tonight. We are all going to the

Hungaria for dinner to celebrate. He's bringing his wife and children along, too.'

'I couldn't be more delighted,' she told him truthfully, aware that the kiss which had meant more than anything in the world to her, had been entirely forgotten by him. She understood, but she was still a little saddened.

'I shall stay here with Stephan and have a quiet evening, but I'll expect you to tell me all about it on our way back to Vienna.'

His eyes opened wide with indignation. 'You will do no such thing. You're going to join us this evening.'

Stubbornly she shook her head. 'Gregor, it's a family occasion, something really special, and I'm only too pleased it's taking place.'

'Stephan is family and you're in charge of him. You will come,' he added in a tone which brooked no further argument.

Happily she smiled and he got to his feet. 'It's as well I have no further commitments whilst I'm here; I'm not used to so much excitement, or for that matter, champagne during the day. All I could elicit from an orchestra just now is a terrible noise.'

She laughed and as he reached the door, he paused to say, 'Put on your best dress tonight, Megan. This is going to be a great occasion.'

As the door closed behind him she reckoned that it would indeed be something special. For her it would be another memory to keep by her in the future when the closest she was likely to get to him would be a seat in the auditorium of the Festival Hall on one of his all too rare visits to London.

★   ★   ★

When she put Stephan to bed that evening he was most concerned about the plane Gregor had promised to buy him.

'If your uncle has made a promise, he will certainly keep it,' she assured him.

'And then you will be able to take it in the square or the Volksgarten and fly it as often as you wish.'

With that possibility in view Stephan fell asleep smiling, oblivious to the drama of the day.

Megan realised that, although she was hanging on to every moment she shared with Gregor as something infinitely precious, she was falling more deeply in love with him. It was one thing to idolise so famous and talented a person, but quite another to love a man who had suffered so much and was scarred by it.

When he came to her suite she was ready and no one could have guessed her inner longings, so successfully did she hide them. She didn't doubt that all his longings at that moment were centred on his brother.

'A sack-load of mail arrived for you this evening,' she told him briskly as the car set off for the restaurant.'As I'm travelling with you as your secretary, it was delivered to my suite.'

'I'm glad about that. I shall deal with it another time. The champagne made me fall asleep the moment I got back to my suite, so I wouldn't have welcomed the interruption.'

'The rest will have done you good.'

He gave her an amused look and put his hand over hers. 'It would be good to have someone like you fussing over me all the time. If only you knew about International Law, I could engage you exclusively as my legal adviser.'

'I'm not sure I would like that, Gregor,' she answered in an unsteady voice.

He withdrew his hand. 'I'm sure you wouldn't.'

It took them only a few minutes to reach the restaurant in the heart of Pest, and as they got out of the car Megan glanced up at the facade. The restaurant looked as plush and opulent as any she had seen.

'My mother always told me this place was the centre of café society before the war when kings and courtesans mingled here with giants of the literary world,' he told her as he instructed the driver when to return.

When they went inside Megan was even more amazed to see that the place had been restored to its old baroque magnificence. Tables nestled between gilded columns which supported wrought iron balconies and waiters in white tie and tails scurried to a fro, serving the many diners.

When Gregor gave his name to the head waiter he was handed an envelope. Megan transferred her attention back to him, looking curiously at the envelope. It might have been another letter from an admirer of his work, but somehow she doubted it and felt uneasy.

He tore it open quickly and scanned the page before giving vent to what was obviously an Hungarian oath which caused the head waiter to raise his eyebrows.

Megan put one hand on Gregor's arm. 'What is it? What has happened? It's Emil, isn't it?'

Gregor stared unseeingly ahead into the restaurant where so many people were enjoying themselves. 'He can't come.'

She shook her head. 'Why ever not?'

He drew in a sharp breath as he screwed the letter into a ball in his fist. 'It seems he has been sent to Gyor on urgent business.'

'That seems to be rather a coincidence, coming just at this time.'

'More than that,' he answered grimly. 'It's a piece of petty spite over something which happened twenty-five years ago.'

Once again her heart ached for him. It was doubly cruel after so many years apart.

'I'm so sorry, Gregor. This is an awful thing to have happened, but we can't keep standing here; we'd better go back to the hotel.'

He put out his hand to stop her making for the door. 'No.' She paused to cast him a curious look. 'There is a table waiting for us; we'll stay. After all, we still have something to celebrate.'

Giving him an uncertain look, she followed the head waiter to their table. Outwardly as he consulted the menu and advised her as to the dishes available, he displayed no sign of the bitter disappointment he must have been feeling.

When they'd given their order she asked in a whisper, 'What are you going to do?'

'There is very little I can do, unfortunately.'

'Are you going to wait here in Budapest until he comes back?'

'Unfortunately I can't. I have commitments in Salzburg which can't be put off any longer.'

She looked dismayed. 'But when will you have the opportunity to see him again, Gregor?'

He gazed across the table at her and then to her relief he smiled. 'You're frowning. Such concern,' he mocked gently.

Abashed she lowered her eyes. 'I

can't help myself; I know in your place I'd be devastated.'

'You needn't be. I will see him again — next time I come to Hungary.'

Her hands clenched into fists on the table top. 'Oh, it's just so unfair. You came so close.'

He continued to smile in the face of her outrage. 'So many years have come between us, Megan, a little while longer does not matter. For the moment it's enough to know he's alive and well. It's everything after the years I despaired of ever finding him.'

She let out a long breath. 'I know, but your attitude, I find, is marvellous. I'm afraid I couldn't be so patient.'

'You would soon learn to be in such circumstances.'

'What will Alexis say when you tell him?'

'Naturally he'll be pleased, but, truthfully, it won't mean as much to him. He cannot remember Emil at all, so meeting him will be like seeing a stranger.'

Her eyes clouded with pain. 'It hardly bears thinking about; families being split up like yours.'

He shrugged. 'In Europe it's not unusual. In my own world of music I know a great many refugees who may or may not have families alive in their homeland.'

She gave him a curious look. 'What is Alexis like?'

His eyes opened wide. 'Did you never meet him?'

She smiled sadly. 'I was only fifteen years old when my sister got married.'

'I think I can safely say you would like Alexis. All women like him. He is very handsome and personable.'

Megan laughed then. 'That's no surprise, knowing my sister.' Her smile faded. 'My parents refused to come to the wedding, as you probably know, and by the time I was old enough to come by myself, Vivien was back in London and well on her way to being divorced.'

'I don't blame your parents for

disapproving. I wasn't too pleased about it myself. They had their heads in the clouds, in love with the idea of love. Truly, Alexis hasn't changed at all; he's still a little boy at heart. It's not his fault, though; I always had my music so our mother spoiled him terribly. I suppose it was to make up for all he had missed. Afterwards, when I was earning more money than we were used to, I indulged him, too.'

'That might well be true, Gregor, but at the time of the wedding my parents didn't know what Alexis was like — they didn't trouble to find out — and they couldn't have known it wouldn't last. My mother, I think, was just furious because she'd always planned a great white wedding at our local church with a hundred guests and all the trimmings. She has never forgiven Vivien for cheating her out of that. At the time, at that age, I thought it was all marvellously romantic and hated to miss it.'

'Perhaps your mother will get her

wish when it's your turn.'

Her cheeks flushed with embarrassment and she was forced to look away, so it came as a relief and a distraction when the waiter arrived with their wine; Tokay to drink with the hors d'oeuvre of delicately smoked fish, and then a red wine for the main course which was pork spiced with paprika.

'This must bring back a lot of memories,' she murmured as he sampled the wine and found it to his satisfaction.

'Yes, the food certainly does. My mother always cooked in the Hungarian way, but over the past few years I have grown used to eating the food of whatever country I happen to be in.'

They'd just begun to eat the main course when a gypsy trio began to move around the restaurant, pausing at each table to play traditional Magyar folk tunes.

'This certainly isn't part of the Hungarian way of life,' he said, laughingly when they approached their table. 'This is strictly for visitors.'

'But charming all the same,' she replied.

'Very much so,' he agreed, tipping the leader so generously they stayed to play several tunes.

As the gypsies played Megan gazed at him across the table. She had been shattered that Emil had not been able to come, yet a treacherous being deep inside her rejoiced at having him to herself.

'You lead a marvellously exciting life,' she told him as the trio moved on to another table at last.

'I admit I enjoy it,' he answered philosophically, 'but it can be a lonely existence at times. All those hotels begin to look alike wherever they happen to be. My one excursion into marriage proved it's a folly to try to share such a nomadic existence with someone else.'

'Didn't she want to go with you?'

'At first, but then she grew bored by sitting around hotels whilst I rehearsed for hours on end.'

Breathlessly as she took another sip of wine, she said, 'Not all women are like that. There must be many who could share such a life with you.'

He smiled faintly and lifted up his wine glass, staring into it as if fascinated. 'But who would, perhaps, not wish to.'

Megan knew he was thinking of Francesca Lamarti. What a wonderful couple they would make. Two great talents. But perhaps Francesca was enough of a realist to suspect their talents might equally lead to inevitable friction. Megan was now in a position where she could sympathise with his longing.

To cover her confusion she sipped at the wine, laughing as she did so, 'Such a terrible name for so good a wine.'

'Do you know how it came to be known as Bull's Blood?' She shook her head and he refilled her glass. 'It was called that by the Turks when they invaded Hungary centuries ago.

178

Although their religion forbade them to drink alcohol at all they found this very palatable, so one day when they were discovered drinking the wine by someone in authority, one of them declared that they were not drinking wine at all but bull's blood.'

She gulped back some of the wine. When she looked at him again she drew in a sharp breath. 'Your visit has been a great success, Gregor.'

He looked pensive for a moment or two before answering, 'Yes, I believe I can consider it so. Because it's my birthplace that is more satisfying than usual. When I return to Austria, I must concentrate on Salzburg and *Lucia*, but,' he added, glancing at her, 'I have enjoyed this little interlude.'

'So have I,' she responded with more enthusiasm than she intended, and because of it she blushed. 'And after Salzburg?'

'Franzi and I go to Paris to record the entire opera.'

A shaft of what could only be

described as jealousy cut through her at the thought of them in Paris together.

'I must buy it when it becomes available,' she told him, returning her attention to her wine in order to hide her feelings from him.

'I shall send you a copy.'

She smiled sadly, gazing down at the tablecloth, pristine in its whiteness. 'By then you'll have forgotten all about me.'

He looked at her in surprise before smiling. 'Do you really think so? After sharing so much together these past few days?'

She looked away in confusion and he went on, heedlessly, 'What a pity I'm not planning to come to London. We could have had dinner together and reminisced about your unplanned visit.'

She looked up at him again, her eyes bleak. 'But you're not coming, are you?'

He cast her a regretful smile. 'No. After Paris I shall come back to Vienna for the autumn season and then when Christmas is over, I'm going to the United States for a series of concerts.'

He leaned forward as the waiter removed their plates. 'We seem to spend a great deal of time talking about me. Let's talk about you for a change.'

She shook her head in embarrassment. 'I'm not at all interesting, Gregor. I live a very mundane life.'

'Let me be the judge of that, young woman. Tell me what you do; save desperate men from the gallows?'

She laughed at that. 'We don't have one any more, as I'm sure you know very well. My work at the university leaves me with plenty of time so I work in a law centre where people can get free advice when they can't otherwise afford to pay for it.'

'It sounds like a good idea. You're very kind to give your time and talents to such a venture.'

'Well, my job pays me well enough for my needs and, like you, I enjoy the variety.'

He hesitated a moment before asking, 'And men? Who is the man in your life?'

She lowered her eyes, for his were probing and she was afraid they would give her away. She had never had to hide her feelings before in this way, and was quite unused to subterfuge.

'There must be at least one,' he probed and she looked at him at last, 'If not a score.'

'Yes, there is one,' she answered breathlessly at last.

He gazed at her for a long moment before saying, 'He is a very lucky fellow. Tell him so from me.'

The irony of that statement made her laugh, harshly, as he drained his glass of the last drop of wine. 'Somehow I don't think he would believe me.'

'Do you want some dessert?'

She was glad of the change of subject and answered with a slight gasp, 'I couldn't eat another morsel.'

He pushed back his chair. 'Then I think we should go back to the hotel.'

Although Megan knew the evening would have to end sometime she was, even so, reluctant for it to do so.

Tomorrow they would be back in Vienna and he would become preoccupied with the coming Festival. Because of that she would see little of him once again, and before long nothing at all.

As he came round to her side of the table she felt nothing but sorrow at her own loss.

10

'It really has been a most remarkable trip,' Gregor announced as they drove back towards Vienna from the airport the following morning.

Silently, Megan agreed, but her reasons were totally different to his.

'You won't forget about the plane,' Stephan reminded him. 'The one that flies on its own.'

'That's rude,' Megan scolded but Gregor only laughed.

'It's all right. All children are the same.'

'I only know Stephan.'

His manner sobered. 'Me, too.' Then he looked at the boy again. 'I will remember to buy it, Stephan, I promise.'

'Your Papa might be waiting for you when we arrive back,' she told the child, ruffling his hair.

'He won't believe where we've been.'

'You will have to tell him all about it,' Gregor pointed out, 'including the fact you have found a new uncle.'

'Will he come to visit us in Vienna?'

'One day I hope he will. Perhaps we can arrange it for the next time you come to visit us.'

'And will you come, too, Aunt Megan?'

In his innocence the child had reminded her of what was both inevitable and painful and when she replied her voice was a little husky.

'When your Papa is here, there is no need for me to be.'

'Your aunt is longing to go back to her very important work,' Gregor pointed out, and although she looked to him, seeking any irony in his manner, she could detect none. 'It would be unfair of us to detain her.'

'It's not such important work,' the boy said sulkily. 'Mummy always says she can't understand why Aunt Megan isn't bored silly by it.'

At such a breach of confidence Megan and Gregor exchanged looks over his head and then burst out laughing.

When the car drew up outside the house at last, it seemed to Megan a much longer time than the three days they'd actually been away.

As Gregor got out of the car he said, 'I must go immediately and look through my mail before I telephone Franzi. Let's hope she is fully recovered by now. We need to rehearse that opera in earnest from now on.'

'When you go to Salzburg you'll be staying there, won't you?' she asked, making a great fuss of getting Stephan out of the car in order to cover her own uncertainty.

'At least until the day after the performance, but possibly longer. It's a great meeting place for those connected with music. Unless it's absolutely essential it's a pity to leave earlier than necessary.'

Frau Hemmel was at the door to

greet them. 'Welcome home, Maestro. I hope the concert went well.'

'It was a great success, Frau Hemmel,' he responded good-naturedly, and it was impossible for anyone to tell what a nerve-shattering experience his visit had turned out to be.

Stephan went streaking up the stairs, past them all. Megan called him back and he reluctantly took charge of his small suitcase, carrying it up with him rather less enthusiastically this time.

Megan noticed that a telegram was lying on a table which stood just inside the doorway.

When Gregor asked in German, 'Has anything important happened whilst I've been away? Any urgent messages?' the housekeeper reached for it.

'This arrived yesterday, Maestro. I hope it isn't too important as I didn't think I should open it.'

Megan looked on as he ripped open the envelope. 'Ah, at last.' He glanced at her for a moment or two before saying, 'It's from Alexis; he's coming home.'

Whereas once she would have greeted this news with relief, the inevitable only served to subdue her.

'Where has he been all this time?'

'What does it matter? He's coming, that's the important thing. He's having to change planes at Frankfurt, but he'll be home any time now.'

'From where?' she insisted. 'I thought it said New York on that telegram.'

He drew a sigh of resignation. 'You are very observant, persistent, too. Are you always like this?'

'Yes; it was how I was trained to be,' she answered dryly. 'I thought you told me he'd left New York by the time I arrived here.'

He subjected her to one of his charming smiles which she immediately mistrusted. 'He must have returned.'

Megan frowned. 'Isn't that rather odd, Gregor? I mean, you would really think he'd have got one of your messages in one of the other places he visits long before now. You don't think he deliberately ignored your messages, do you?'

'No, I don't.' She continued to look at him questioningly and then he drew yet another sigh. 'Very well, if you must know, I never tried to contact him at all.'

Her mouth opened as if she were about to say something and then it closed again.

At last she managed to ask, 'Why, Gregor? Why on earth did you lie to me?'

'It was only a white lie,' he begged, looking amused and almost childlike.

'In my view a lie is a lie,' she told him heatedly. 'I can't understand why you bothered.'

'It was for the very best of reasons.' He paused before adding, 'I found you interesting enough to want you to stay a little while longer. It's quite simple really.'

Once again she was speechless and then there came the sound of running feet above their heads. Stephan's face appeared over the baluster rail.

'Aunt Meg! Uncle Gregor! Mummy's here! Mummy's actually here in Vienna. Isn't that super!'

All else was forgotten as both Gregor and Megan looked at each other in alarm.

'Vivien can't be here,' she gasped. 'There must be some mistake.'

'Stephan must know his own mother,' Gregor retorted, equally shocked.

'I am so sorry, Maestro,' the house-keeper apologised, 'but Frau Davos arrived a short time before you.'

The three of them marched up the stairs to find that Vivien was indeed ensconced in the large salon. As they came into the room she disentangled herself from Stephan's importuning and sauntered across the floor towards them, her face a wreath of smiles. Megan didn't doubt she was enjoying the consternation and surprise her arrival had caused.

'Hi. I can see this is something of a surprise — for all of us.'

She glanced at Gregor and when she spoke to him her voice was an octive lower. 'Hello, Gregor. It's been a long time since we last met.'

'Hello, Vivien,' he responded with a coolness she just couldn't ignore. 'What brings you here?'

Vivien threw back her head. 'A longing for old Vienna, of course. I have some *very* happy memories of my stay here.'

She cast him an arch look as he said, rather abruptly, 'Frau Hemmel, bring these ladies some tea. I have some telephone calls to make so you will have to excuse me.'

Without another word he turned on his heel and strode out of the room, watched in dismay by Megan. For some reason she couldn't recognise, she didn't want to be left alone with her sister.

'Oh, for heaven's sake don't make tea,' Vivien told Frau Hemmel who was also about to leave the room. 'Tea is so awful in this country. May we have some coffee instead?'

'And lemonade for me,' Stephan added.

'You can't expect Frau Hemmel to bring it up here for you,' Vivien scolded. 'Go along with her, Stephan, and I'm sure she'll let you have a nice big glass full of lemonade.'

The child was quite happy to do so and when the door had closed behind them Vivien gave her a mocking look before going to the sofa and taking a cigarette pack from her bag. Megan watched her as she went, her hips, in a figure-hugging, dress swinging seductively. As she casually tipped out a cigarette Megan felt her heart fill with fury.

As Vivien fumbled in her bag for a lighter she said, 'Well, well, who'd have thought I would find you so cosily tucked up here?'

As she inhaled deeply Megan threw her own bag down on the sofa. 'Never mind about me; what are you doing here?'

She smiled without a semblance of mirth. 'I am, so to speak, part of the family.'

'I take leave to doubt that your ex-husband would agree with that, but you know exactly what I mean. You went to Los Angeles. That is why I'm here. Didn't you get the part, after all?'

Vivien flicked ash into an ashtray. 'As a matter of fact, I did, but filming doesn't begin for another eight weeks and as I don't know anyone over there I decided to come back.'

'What about your pet producer? Wasn't he there with you?'

She made a grimace as she crushed out the cigarette. 'His wife was waiting for him at the airport. Apparently, when he's at home she hugs him very close to her bosom. That didn't leave much time for me.' She cast Megan another mocking glance. 'You seem rather put out by my arrival.'

Her sister shrugged, sorry that it was so apparent. 'I'm surprised, that's all.'

Vivien sat down on the sofa and

spread both arms out along the back, smiling now. 'This place is just the same. I'd almost forgotten how big and empty it always seemed.' Megan made no reply. 'Gregor doesn't change either. That devastating Hungarian fire is still simmering away inside him. I dare say you've noticed.'

Megan didn't like the sarcasm, which was evident in her manner, especially when it nudged so closely to the truth. 'I wasn't aware you knew him so well.'

Vivien merely grinned before asking, 'Where is Alexis? The housekeeper was going on about him not being here, which is apparent anyway, but do you know where he is?'

'At this very moment he's on his way back from New York.'

Her sister's eyes grew suddenly cold. 'And more to the point, why are you still here? When I arrived back in London I rang your flat to check that everything was all right. There was no reply so I thought I'd do the next best thing and ring through to Alexis to make sure Stephan had arrived safely. Imagine my surprise when the housekeeper told me that Alexis hadn't been here in months and that you, Stephan and Gregor were in, of all places, Budapest. Really, Megan, I just had to hop on a plane and find out for myself what it was all about.'

'You didn't send the telegram, so no one here expected our arrival. I had to stay because there was no one else to look after your son. It's that simple.'

She looked doubtful. 'Is it, Meg? All three of you looked remarkably cosy. From what I can see, you've really made yourself at home here.'

'I had no choice.'

Vivien cast her another disbelieving look and then reached for a newspaper which she thrust at her sister. 'I've been reading that whilst waiting for someone to arrive.'

Megan looked down at it in bewilderment to see her own face staring back at her. The captioned photograph had been taken at the President's reception and it was too prominently placed to miss.

'What does it say? My German is restricted to *Bitte* and *Danke*.'

Vivien took the paper from her and began to read in a high, bright and gossipy voice. '*Who is the attractive brunette on the arm of the dashing Davos? He is not saying but we have it on firm authority the lady is staying at the Davos house in Vienna whilst Lamarti is indisposed in Salzburg.*'

She threw the paper down again and Megan sighed, realising, of course, that Gregor himself must have seen it, and no doubt Francesca Lamarti, too. How angry they must be, yet Gregor must have known gossip was bound to ensue when so famous a personality was seen with an unknown woman.

Vivien continued to look at her disbelievingly. 'Oh, Meg, who do you think you're fooling? We're sisters, remember. We grew up together. I saw the way you looked at him.'

Megan's eyes opened wide in alarm.

'Don't be idiotic, Vivien,' she protested.

Her sister smiled. 'You're not alone, I assure you. Gregor has quite a legion of adoring females who will never believe all that Hungarian passion and continental charm is strictly for fun. He never fails, does he? You're way out of your league this time, my love. You're just a little lamb and Gregor is very much the big bad wolf.'

'You don't know what you're talking about! I don't really care if you think me that stupid but please don't slander Gregor with thoughts and feelings which simply aren't there.'

Megan was angry, but her sister refused to be riled. 'Where Gregor is concerned I certainly do know what I'm talking about. Tell me, Meg, who do you think was responsible for my marriage breaking up?'

For a moment Vivien's words went round in her head and then she came back towards her. 'Not Gregor?'

She nodded smilingly. 'I grant you he's not a man a woman ever forgets and I have certainly known a few. So you see, dear sister, the saintly Gregor is human after all.'

Megan stared at her in disbelief. It was something which had never occurred to her. Gregor and Francesca she could understand and accept, but not Vivien. Not his brother's wife.

Furious that she had ever believed him to be above other men, she strode out of the room and slammed the door behind her, almost bumping into Frau Hemmel who was bringing their coffee.

Megan murmured her apologies through her tears and rushed to her own room. Once inside she let the tears flow unchecked until there were no more left and her grief was spent. She felt as betrayed as if she and Gregor had been lovers.

11

Time had lost any meaning. Megan had been lying on the bed, staring at the ceiling for a long time, she knew. After a while she began to get up, aware that there were things to be done.

Slowly, and almost painfully, she stood up and went to the bathroom, washing her face more thoroughly than was necessary to remove the tear stains. It was as if she were trying to wash away her love for Gregor. Whatever it achieved the pain certainly remained.

As she dried her face she studied it carefully in the mirror. Outwardly her appearance had not changed, but she knew she was different now. The lingering naïvety was gone for ever. She had learned a great deal in a short time, which reminded her suddenly of something her father had said when she got her law degree.

'Don't think because you've got that piece of paper you know everything now. There are some things which have to be learned by experience.'

Now she understood more what he had meant. Although hopeless love was a sobering experience, on reflection she would not have missed it for the world. Her love for Gregor Davos was unblighted by Vivien's revelations and would last in her consciousness for all time, and she could not help but be enriched by it.

After a while she picked up her suitcase, opened it and began to throw in all those belongings she hadn't taken with her to Budapest. There were few enough and she'd soon finished.

She had just put the case on the floor when someone knocked on the door. As there was no one she wished to speak to just then she ignored it and hoped whoever it was would go away.

A moment later, however, Vivien's voice reached her through the closed door. 'Meg, I know you're in there, so please let me in.'

Again she ignored her sister, but not to be put off Vivien opened the door which Megan now regretted not locking. Just then she hated Vivien and that was an unfamiliar emotion.

'I knew you were in here. Why didn't you answer?'

Still keeping her back to her, Megan answered, 'Because I wanted to be on my own.'

'It's not like you to sulk.' She drew a sigh. 'I'm sorry if I upset you, Meg, but you really can't go around blinkered. For all that you're a career girl and living in the world like everyone else you are pretty naïve. What I told you was really for the best. He'd only hurt you if you let things develop and I don't believe you've got the sort of strength to withstand it.'

'Thanks for the consideration, Vivien, but I can assure you there was nothing to develop.'

Her sister glanced at the suitcase. 'You haven't unpacked your things yet.'

Megan opened her handbag and began to count her money. 'On the contrary, I've just packed all my things. I'm leaving just as soon as I can get a booking on a plane going to London.'

'Do you have to leave so soon? I mean, I'm sure there's no need for you to rush off like this.'

Megan cast her a cold look before closing her handbag with a decided snap. 'I've done what was asked of me. I was only here to look after Stephan whilst there was no one else to do it. With his father on his way and you here, too, I'm rather superfluous.'

Vivien walked over to the window and stared out on to the Ringstrasse. 'Oh, no doubt I shall be leaving before long, too, just as soon as Alex arrives. It's a good opportunity for us to discuss Stephan.'

'It's not before time.'

Her sister sighed. 'It hasn't been so necessary before. My career is becoming more demanding now. I can't always be available during school holidays — and neither can you — so Alex will have to take more responsibility for him in the future.'

Megan looked at her in astonishment before saying, 'You must be the most selfish mother of all time.'

Vivien's eyes grew wide. 'What do you mean?'

'You and Alex will have to stop passing Stephan around like a football. He's a human being, you know.'

Her sister stiffened with indignation. 'And I am an actress. Stephan is not neglected because of it!'

'Oh, yes, he is. Gregor and I have had to look after him despite *our* demanding careers, but he needs his parents, Vivien. At least one of you all the time, not just school for three-quarters of the year and whoever can spare a few days in between. A child cannot be brought up that way.'

'Well, what would you do in my place?' she demanded.

'If I were lucky enough to have a child like Stephan I would give up everything to look after him, and you really don't have to go so far. Just accept work which coincides when he's at school.'

'It doesn't work out so simply,' she answered, waving her hand irritably in the air, 'and this really is a change of heart for you.' She put her hands on her hips. 'A few weeks looking after an eight-year-old and you're an expert on children. You never fail to amaze me.'

'I'm not an expert on anything, but I have come to know your son. He won't be a child for ever; you can surely spend the time with him until he's grown up and independent.'

'You're joking! The film and stage world has a notoriously bad memory.'

'Well, nevertheless you do have a child and he is your responsibility.'

'Not just mine. Alex must take more responsibility, too.'

'I agree. He's no better than you in that respect. He should give him more time, too. Stephan is getting to the age when he needs a man's guidance. Can't you see that, Vivien?'

'I can see that my son is perfectly well without my being at his beck and call night and day.'

Megan sighed. 'You'll never understand, will you, Vivien? I feel as if I'm talking to a stone wall. I just can't make you see the truth.'

Her sister walked towards the door and wrenched it open. 'I have an idea. When you're married with a home of your own, and you've given up all you've ever worked towards for the dubious pleasures of domesticity, he can stay with you, seeing you're so concerned.'

'I am and he can,' Megan retorted, still angry.

'Until then I suggest that you mind your own business.'

When she'd gone, Megan let out a cry of exasperation and slammed the door shut again, sinking down on the bed and shaking with frustration.

★　★　★

Megan came out of the study and closed the door carefully, almost stealthily. Having done so she began to move away but gasped when she came face to face with a stranger who was looking at her with a mixture of curiosity and amusement.

She, however, suffered no such curiosity; she knew exactly who the blonde and blue eyed stranger must be.

When he said something to her in German she replied, 'You must be Alexis.'

He looked ever more amused. 'You have the advantage of me, *fraulein*. My brother certainly hasn't been lonely in my absence.'

Megan brushed aside the innuendo irritably. 'I'm Megan Amery.' His eyes narrowed and the name obviously stirred some memory in him. 'Vivien's sister.'

His face cleared. 'Ah, yes. I recall she had a little sister, always with her nose in a book. Isn't that right?'

206

She blushed slightly. 'That was a long time ago.'

The look he gave her caused her colour to deepen even further. 'Oh, yes, I can see that.' Suddenly he looked puzzled again. 'But what are you doing here in Vienna? In this house?'

Unaccountably her voice was uneven as she replied, 'I brought Stephan and stayed with him because you weren't here.'

She said it almost accusingly, as if falling in love with Gregor was his fault.

'*You* have brought Stephan? Where is his mother?'

'Actually, she's here now,' Megan replied, feeling acutely uncomfortable. 'She has just arrived, too.'

He was beginning to look even more bewildered. 'And what is *she* doing here?'

'I believe she wishes to talk with you — about Stephan.'

He nodded thoughtfully before he sighed. 'However distasteful that might be, I shall go now and get it over with.

The sooner we talk, the quicker she will be able to leave.' He inclined his head. 'Excuse me, *fraulein*. Let us hope we meet again soon.'

Megan watched him go, her heart heavy. How strange it seemed to her for love to go so completely and to be replaced by hostility.

She stiffened automatically on hearing a footstep on the stairs and it was a great relief for her to see that it was Frau Hemmel, for she feared coming face to face with Gregor. That was something she couldn't bear just then. It was best to savour the memories she had of him and not think of him as the kind of man who would help to break up his brother's marriage.

'Frau Hemmel, I'm leaving now. There's a seat on this afternoon's flight to London and I wondered if you'd be good enough to order a taxi for me.'

The housekeeper looked bewildered. 'So much coming and going! Always I try to keep the house quiet for the Maestro.'

Megan smiled faintly. 'Never mind. Within a few days everything will return to normal.'

'Megan?'

She turned on her heel, gasping a little when she saw Gregor coming towards her. He'd changed his clothes since she'd last seen him and he was carrying a suitcase, but she wasn't sure whether it was the one he had brought from Budapest or another.

He gave her a puzzled look as she said in a bright voice, 'I was just asking Frau Hemmel to ring for a taxi. I've managed to get a seat on the next flight to London.'

His expression revealed no surprise or sorrow. 'So soon?' he asked in a soft voice.

Her smile was ironic now. 'There is no good reason for me to stay any more. Vivien is here and Alexis, too.'

'You've met him?' he asked in some surprise.

'Only for a few minutes.'

'He's with Vivien, discussing their

son rather noisily, from what I could hear.'

'Let's hope they can resolve the situation to Stephan's advantage.'

He looked at his housekeeper then and said, 'It's all right, Frau Hemmel; I'll attend to this matter.'

The woman hurried away, no doubt anxious to reorganise her kitchen to accommodate the extra guests. Feeling awkward now, she was alone with him, Megan watched Frau Hemmel progress down the stairs.

'So,' he said, giving her an assessing look, 'it appears you would have left without even saying goodbye.'

She pushed back her hair and, still not looking at him, she answered, 'You were busy and I have to hurry if I'm to catch that plane.'

'I can take you to the airport.'

That was precisely what she didn't want and immediately began to protest. 'No, no, a taxi will do fine. I don't want to put you to any trouble.'

'You won't. I'm going there myself.'

She did look at him then, her eyes wide and he went on to explain, 'I'm going to Salzburg now.'

'So Signorina Lamarti has recovered?'

'Yes, she is perfectly well and it's very necessary for us to get down to work to perfect the opera.' He looked around. 'Where is your luggage?'

She pointed to where she had left it outside the study and he picked it up along with his own and as he did so he looked at her again.

'The car is waiting outside and we don't want you to miss that flight, do we?'

After hesitating a moment she preceded him down the stairs. When they were ensconced inside the car he said as they emerged into the Ringstrasse, 'Say your goodbyes to Vienna, Megan. Will you miss her?'

She stared down at her clenched hands. 'Yes. Vienna's a lovely city. I shall always remember my stay here.'

The car passed the Opera House and

took the road out of the city. After a few minutes she said impetuously, to fill the onerous silence, 'Before I left I tried to talk to Vivien about Stephan. She wouldn't listen to me, I'm afraid. She doesn't seem to care that he needs a settled home to come to during the school holidays.'

He cast her a sympathetic look and put his arm along the back of the seat, which caused her to shrink into the corner. The memory of being held close in his arms was still very fresh in her mind.

'There is nothing you or I can do about it — for the moment. I have some ideas about him for the future.'

She gave him a look which was a mixture of curiosity and resentment. The last industrial suburbs of Vienna were speeding past and she experienced a great feeling of loss.

'Does Vivien know about it?'

He laughed. 'We haven't discussed it.'

Megan stared out of the window. 'She told me about what happened between you two.'

He seemed to move ever so slightly nearer, looking at her earnestly. 'Really? What did she tell you, I wonder?'

'She told me about the affair you had, when she was still married to Alexis.'

There was a momentary silence when all that could be heard was the hum of the car's engine, and then he answered slowly, 'How odd. I wasn't aware that we'd had an affair, and I usually have a good memory for such matters.'

Irritated by his denial, which only seemed to compound the wrong she answered, 'You needn't think I care what happened.'

'Of course not. Why should you care?' When she didn't answer he went on, 'Needless to say it wasn't because Vivien didn't flirt hard enough, or even because I didn't find her attractive, but however many faults I have I did recall that she was my brother's wife and their marriage was shaky enough at the time.'

She looked at him then to meet a pair

of eyes filled with amusement. 'I can see you don't believe me.'

'Yes, I do, of course I do, but why would she pretend?'

'You tell me.'

Once again she was forced to look away and he said, 'You'll be delighted to leave all this behind and get back to your work in London, and, of course, that man who is so special to you.'

She frowned. 'Man?'

'Yes, the one you told me about when we were in Budapest.'

She nodded. 'Oh, him.' She looked down at her clasped hands again. 'He's not in London and I don't think I'll be seeing so much of him in the future.'

All too soon the airport was ahead of them. She didn't recall it being so near on other occasions. The car paused at traffic lights and Megan knew that within a very few minutes the time would come to bid him a final farewell, and panic began to rise inside her. She wondered if they would shake hands or perhaps he might just casually wave, with his mind already anticipating a reunion with his beloved Franzi.

Megan found that her palms were damp and involuntarily, much to her frustration, tears insisted on welling up in her eyes, something which caused her to keep them averted. That was until she realised that the car had driven right past the passenger terminal and was heading for the far side of the tarmac where the plane for Salzburg was waiting.

Her head snapped up then. 'Gregor! Where are we going? I need to be left at the passenger terminal!'

She watched it shrink into the distance with growing dismay. Gregor made no attempt, however, to alert the driver. Instead he put his hand over hers.

'You don't really want to go back to London, do you?'

'Of course I do!'

His eyes were filled with amusement again. 'Come to Salzburg with me.'

Her mind was reeling, her heart

beating fast. 'Why?'

'Because I want you to.'

'I can't imagine why,' she retorted. 'You don't need me. Signorina Lamarti is waiting for you in Salzburg.'

'What has Franzi to do with it? I'm not asking you to take her place as *Lucia*.' She stared at him and he went on, 'I have taken a suite at the best hotel in Salzburg for the duration of the Festival, and I have always thought it would make an ideal honeymoon hotel. I'm sure you'll agree with me about that when you see it for yourself.'

Her mouth went dry as the car drew up near where the aeroplane was waiting.

'Honeymoon,' she echoed.

'If you're willing to tolerate a little negligence so early in our marriage, we can be married before the Festival begins. Don't you realise I'm in love with you? I'd have thought it would be quite obvious to you by now.'

She just kept on staring at him in

astonishment, hardly daring to believe her ears.

'Of course, I'm not offering an easy life,' he went on, raising her hand to his lips. 'It can be a nomadic one at times and I'm very possessive so I would want you with me . . . '

'I want that, too,' she answered breathlessly at last. 'I love you, too, Gregor.'

'That is all I want to know.'

He raised her hand to his lips again as she said, gazing at him with love and awe, 'I could hardly bear the thought of parting with you. My life would have been totally empty in the future.'

Regardless of the driver who waited patiently to open the car door for them, Gregor took her into his arms and kissed her much as he had done in Budapest, only this time it was for their own pleasure and not for any onlooker. His lips caressed hers, and then her cheeks, her eyes and her neck.

When at last she did draw away she said uncertainly, still breathless, 'What will Franzi say?'

'Why is she so important to you?' he asked, amazed at her insistence.

'Because she is so important to you.'

His look was an indulgent one. 'I think you have the wrong idea about Franzi and me.'

Her mouth was dry. 'I would like to hear about it from you; please, Gregor.'

'You can be certain she'll be delighted when she hears our news. It was Franzi, remember who was always putting you in my way. I'm sure she'll be only too pleased to be a witness at our wedding.'

'I'm not really concerned about her feelings for you. It's what you feel for her which concerns me. You loved her.'

'I dare say I always will, but,' he added when she looked crestfallen, 'not the way I love you. There are many different ways to love. My brother, Stephan, Franzi — and the greatest love of all, that of a man for a woman. Franzi and I just used each other to put off those who were likely to become a nuisance with their attentions. She suffers in much the same way as I do, so if everyone is made to believe we are a pair in public, then we are free to do what we please in private.'

Megan drew a sigh and sank back in the seat. 'So much anguish for nothing.'

His lips brushed against her briefly again. 'Anguish is never in vain, my love. It ensures we can savour the sweetness all the more.'

He took her hand and helped her out of the car and with their arms about each other walked towards the plane which would not only take them to Salzburg, but to a new future — together.

THE END

We do hope that you have enjoyed reading this large print book.

Did you know that all of our titles are available for purchase?

We publish a wide range of high quality large print books including:
Romances, Mysteries, Classics
General Fiction
Non Fiction and Westerns

Special interest titles available in large print are:
The Little Oxford Dictionary
Music Book, Song Book
Hymn Book, Service Book

Also available from us courtesy of Oxford University Press:
Young Readers' Dictionary
(large print edition)
Young Readers' Thesaurus
(large print edition)

For further information or a free brochure, please contact us at:
Ulverscroft Large Print Books Ltd.,
The Green, Bradgate Road, Anstey,
Leicester, LE7 7FU, England.
Tel: (00 44) **0116 236 4325**
Fax: (00 44) **0116 234 0205**

THREE TALL TAMARISKS

Christine Briscomb

Joanna Baxter flies from Sydney to run her parents' small farm in the Adelaide Hills while they recover from a road accident. But after crossing swords with Riley Kemp, life is anything but uneventful. Gradually she discovers that Riley's passionate nature and quirky sense of humour are capturing her emotions, but a magical day spent with him on the coast comes to an abrupt end when the elegant Greta intervenes. Did Riley love Greta after all?

SUMMER IN HANOVER SQUARE

Charlotte Grey

The impoverished Margaret Lambart is suddenly flung into all the glitter of the Season in Regency London. Suspected by her godmother's nephew, the influential Marquis St. George, of being merely a common adventuress, she has, nevertheless, a brilliant success, and attracts the attentions of the young Duke of Oxford. However, when the Marquis discovers that Margaret is far from wanting a husband he finds he has to revise his estimate of her true worth.

CONFLICT OF HEARTS

Gillian Kaye

Somerset, at the end of World War I: Daniel Holley, unhappily married to an ailing wife and father of four grown-up children, is attracted to beautiful schoolteacher Harriet Bray, but he knows his love is hopeless. Daniel's only daughter, Amy, who dreams of becoming a milliner and is caught up in her love for young bank clerk John Tottle, looks on as the drama of Daniel and Harriet's fate and happiness gradually unfolds.

THE SOLDIER'S WOMAN

Freda M. Long

When Lieutenant Alain d'Albert was deserted by his girlfriend, a replacement was at hand in the shape of Christina Calvi, whose yearning for respectability through marriage did not quite coincide with her profession as a soldier's woman. Christina's obsessive love for Alain was not returned. The handsome hussar married an heiress and banished the soldier's woman from his life. But Christina was unswerving in the pursuit of her dream and Alain found his resistance weakening . . .

THE TENDER DECEPTION

Laura Rose

When Sophia Barton was taken from Curton Workhouse to be a scullery-maid at Perriman Court, her future looked bleak. Was it really an act of Providence that persuaded Lady Perriman to adopt her as her ward? Sophia was brought up together with the Perriman children, and before sailing with his regiment for India, George, the heir to the title, declared his love. But tragedy hit the family and Sophia found herself caught up in a web of mystery and intrigue.

CONVALESCENT HEART

Lynne Collins

They called Romily the Snow Queen, but once she had been all fire and passion, kindled into loving by a man's kiss and sure it would last a lifetime. She still believed it would, for her. It had lasted only a few months for the man who had stormed into her heart. After Greg, how could she trust any man again? So was it likely that surgeon Jake Conway could pierce the icy armour that the lovely ward sister had wrapped about her emotions?